Amalfi Press
Copyright © James Kennedy 2019
ISBN 978-1-9164151-1-9

GW00455899

MURDER IN BROADLAND

James Kennedy

CHAPTER ONE

Dan Cooper drained his pint and rolled another cigarette, lighting it up he walked out of the Horning Swan into the street. The village was packed with holidaymakers most of whom were dressed in shorts and espadrilles. There were also a sprinkling of would be 'admirals' wearing the obligatory peaked caps and blazers. Detective sergeant Cooper allowed himself a wry smile, most of 'em wouldn't know one end of a boat from the other,; weekenders mostly, trying to impress their spouses and other holiday makers. Unlocking his car he drove carefully along the narrow road towards a collection of boatyards just outside the village. The date was the 29th of July 1962, the height of the boating season, which had really taken off since the war and was now a multi million pound business. However in the last three weeks there had been two young girls found dead in suspicious circumstances in the river. His Inspector had been under great pressure to deal with the matter quickly and had of course passed it on.

'Drop everything and get on to this straight away Cooper, time is of the essence and this maniac must be stopped.'
'What manpower can I expect sir?' Cooper inquired.
'I can only spare you three at the moment; I will endeavour to release more as cases are cleared.'
Inwardly Cooper groaned, he had heard that one before, Inspector Grant continued.

2

'I have seconded Medler, Whitlum and young Foley to you. 'he is a bright lad and it will give him experience of detection procedure.'

'There will be a lot of legwork in this sir. I don't think three will be sufficient if you want this clearing up quickly.'

'That will have to do for now Cooper,' We are short handed as it is and with the holiday season in full swing we are at full stretch.' 'I will expect a progress report on my desk each morning Sergeant and remember an early arrest is essential; carry on.'

That was four days ago and Cooper had to admit he was no nearer solving the case than when he had started. He pulled off the road and drove down a muddy track, parking outside a run down boatyard.

Carefully avoiding the mud he picked his way to the office and entered; a harassed looking man in his fifties wearing a blue boiler suit looked up from a desk covered in bills and invoices. Cooper flashed his card and the man looked even more harassed.

'I suppose you're here about the girl,' the man said running his hand through his thinning gray hair.

'That's right sir,' replied Cooper lighting up a cigarette.

The man jerked a thumb at a large notice on the wall; 'these places catch fire very easily, what with the wood dust and varnish and stuff,' he said.

'Sorry,' said Cooper throwing the offending weed out of the door. 'Can you show me where she was found?'

The man led him into the working area where two men were putting the finishing touches to a thirty foot yacht hull. The aromatic smell of timber and varnish was pleasant. He showed him through a side door onto a concrete apron that

3

led to a slipway. A dyke ran down the side of the building and the man pointed to it and said;

'She had been washed into it by passing cruisers probably.'

'Why do you say that?' said Cooper, 'the body could have been dumped there by whoever killed her.'

'No, that couldn't have happened.'

The man paused and a look of sorrow passed across his face. 'You see she had been in contact with the propeller of a boat.'

Cooper was silent for a moment, he had been in such a hurry that he had neglected to consult the pathologist; damn.'

'Who found her?' he asked.

'My brother Brian,' said the man; 'he had gone out to have a 'ciggy' and spotted her lying face down in the water.' 'We fished her out and I called the police.' 'She had been a pretty girl before the river started on her, about twenty something I should think.' 'What sort of maniac could do such a thing?'

'That's a question I've been asking myself ever since I joined the force,' Cooper replied.

'Thanks for your co-operation sir, I may come back if anything else occurs to me'

As he returned to his car he made a mental note to contact the Pathologist and if possible examine the bodies. The trouble was that having been immersed in water vital evidence would be washed away making it virtually impossible to gain any useful information. When he got back to the station there was a note on his desk telling him to report to Inspector Grant. There had been another killing; this time the body had turned up on Breydon Water, a series of mud flats where the Yare and the Bure rivers came out at Yarmouth. Inspector Grant's words were still ringing in Cooper's ears.

'There are people upstairs who think that we should call in Scotland Yard as the local force doesn't seem to be coping.'

That was unfair thought Cooper; trying to solve a murder in an area of high population most of whom are constantly on the move requires more than two constables and a boy. He rolled himself a cigarette and lit it; there had to be some way of tracking down this killer, it just needed a lucky break.

It seemed to him most likely that either the girls were killed on board a boat or they were killed elsewhere and then dumped from the boat; probably whilst on the move at night. He picked up the phone and rang the River Police, speaking to a PC. Stebbings.

'Do you patrol the river at night' he asked? '

'Not usually, unless we've had a tip off about something,' replied Stebbings, 'why do you ask?'

He explained and Stebbings said,

'It's not very likely as navigating the river at night is quite risky.' 'Unless you have a powerful light on the bow you could very easily run aground.'

He thanked the constable and rang off; it seemed he had run into a dead end. This killer seemed to have thought of the perfect way to dispose of his victims without leaving any clue, the girls had been stripped naked before being dumped in the water and any jewelry they had been wearing removed.

Police Cadet Foley came into the office; he looked weary and Cooper waved him into a chair.

'Any luck he asked?'

The boy shook his head,

'We've been covering all the moorings between Horning and Potter Heigham this morning, but it's like looking for a needle in a haystack.'

'I thought I'd cracked the killer's 'modus operandi,' said Cooper. Then went on to describe his conversation with the River Police. Foley thought for a minute and then said,

'He wouldn't need a light if he was wearing Army night goggles; they make it appear as bright as day.'

Cooper sat bolt upright; the boy had hit the nail on the head right enough.

'Are these things easy to obtain Foley?'

'Not easy, but if you had been in the Army you could probably have 'acquired' a pair.'

Cooper was elated; he congratulated the lad on his perception and said, 'before your head gets too swollen nip down to the canteen and get us a coffee.' He walked over to a large map of the Norfolk river system and looked at where the bodies had been found. The first had been taken out of the river at Wroxham, the second from the dyke at Horning and the third had turned up at Breydon; the killer had been traveling down the Bure to Yarmouth. His heart sank as he realized that there were three rivers accessible from Yarmouth and if the boat was sea going a fourth option. There was also the fact that all told there were over two hundred and fifty miles of navigable waterways in Norfolk and Suffolk.

CHAPTER TWO

The previous day he had gone to the morgue to view the bodies and talk to the Pathologist.

'There are several things the bodies have in common' said Mr Merryweather 'firstly there are no signs of a struggle, no skin under the fingernails or bruising consistent with putting up a fight.' 'Secondly they were killed by pressure on the carotid artery.'

D S Cooper looked puzzled 'why is that unusual he asked. Merryman smiled, 'because it is a favorite method used by the military, death occurs in seconds. 'The final thing was that there were no signs of sexual interference'

'What conclusions did you draw from all that,' asked Cooper?

'Apart from the fact that the killer left no forensic evidence, which is remarkable enough in itself, I am drawn to the possibility that our man is either a current or recent member of Special Forces.' Also he is a psychopath who enjoys killing for it's own sake; probably that is the only way he gets sexual satisfaction.'

'Phew, that's quite a lot of information from very little evidence' said Cooper. 'What about the lack of any signs of a struggle?'

'There I must admit I took a leap in the dark said Merryweather.

'I think he used some sort of opiate, but there is nothing in the blood samples or the contents of the stomach in any of them to prove it.'

'You mean he gave them a Micky Finn,' exclaimed Cooper 'how?'

'Probably slipped it in their drink; they all had traces of alcohol in their blood samples.'

'He seems to have thought it all out most carefully,' mused Cooper 'almost like a military campaign.'

'You are dealing with a very dangerous man who will stop at nothing to satisfy his desires and will certainly kill again,' replied Merryweather.

Cooper was very thoughtful as he drove back to the station.

His phone was ringing as he walked into his office and he picked up.

'Hello Guv,' it was Foley.

'Less of the familiarity Foley I am Sergeant Cooper to you' he snapped.

'Sorry Sergeant' said a contrite Foley, "but we've had a breakthrough.'

Cooper felt a surge of elation, 'what have you got, quickly out with it.'

'A witness sir; she and the second girl were mates on holiday.'

'We are bringing her in to the station now.'

Cooper rubbed his hands, this was just the break they needed, at last things are beginning to go our way. He rolled a celebratory cigarette and sat down at his desk to await the arrival of the witness.

Half an hour later Cooper sat in an interrogation room facing Wendy Patterson, a rather vapid unkempt sort of girl.

Her clothes were garish and mismatched and he noticed that her fingernails were bitten. Some people would have rather unkindly rated her as a cheap little tart, but Cooper was not a judgmental sort of person, he merely wanted her evidence.

He sent out for a cup of tea for her and gave her permission to smoke before turning on the recording machine. After asking for her details he asked her about her relationship with the dead girl, whose name was Brenda Gant. Both lived in Chelmsford, had gone to the same school and had been friends for several years. They had decided on a holiday on the Broads and had hired a cruiser from a boatyard in Wroxham. It was a familiar story about looking for boys on holiday and having a good time.

'Tell me about the night that Brenda went missing.'

The girl leaned forward in a confidential manner and said.

'Well we had moored up at Horning for the night as we had heard that there were lots of boys that went to the Ferry to pick up chicks' 'We got there about eight; the place was heaving, there was a band playing and everyone was having a good time. We danced with several different boys, but I paired off with this local guy and we sat down at a table at the back. I looked around for Brenda and saw her sitting at the bar talking to a tall feller with a cropped haircut.' 'We were getting on like a house on fire and he invited me back to his boat; I looked up to see Brenda so I could tell her we were leaving, but she had gone.'

'Can you remember any more details about the man she was with?' interrupted Cooper; 'anything at all?'

'She thought for a moment and said; 'yeah, now I think about it, he had a lovely tan as if he had just come back from somewhere abroad; also he had a scar down his left cheek, it showed up against the tan.'

'Sorry to have stopped you please go on,' Cooper said.

'Well, to cut a long story short I didn't get back to our boat till morning and went on board to find Brenda hadn't returned.' 'I didn't worry much at first 'cos I thought she had clicked and was still with the guy she met the previous night; but when it started to get dark and she still wasn't back I began to get worried.'

'Why didn't you report her missing,' said Cooper?

The girl hesitated and then said. 'Well there had been a previous time that she had spent a week with some guy she met on holiday and didn't bother to tell me.'

He ended the questioning shortly after as she couldn't think of anything more, but asked her if she could help with a photo fit picture of the man. They had to settle for a profile sketch as this was the only side of him she had been able to see.

CHAPTER THREE

Cooper was briefing his three foot soldiers in the information room; which now had the sketch of the left hand profile of the killer in pride of place.

'At least now we have a face to look for' he was saying.

'Well half a face,' mumbled Whitlum disconsolately, Cooper turned to him 'did you have something constructive to add PC Whitlum?'

'No Sarge,' muttered Whitlum looking down at his large boots.

'Look I know you are all having a hard time, 'of course we should have had a lot more men, but the fact is there aren't any to spare at the moment, so it's down to us to get results.'

'If we don't then the 'Super' will call in Scotland Yard and you will be back on the beat and I will probably be directing traffic; so get your fingers out.'

They trooped out in silence and Cooper knew he had a morale problem on his hands. He picked up the phone and rang the Inspector.

'May I come and see you sir, there have been developments that I would like to discuss with you'

There was a pause on the line and then Inspector Grant said, 'very well Cooper I can spare you five minutes.'

He knocked and entered the clinically neat office, Grant sat behind a remarkably clear desk with blotting pad, pens and desk diary all positioned strategically in front of him, Grant waved him to a chair carefully positioned so that whoever sat in it had to look up to the Inspector.

Grant said,'well Cooper what is it?'

'Ther have been developments sir that you should know about.'

'Yes, yes, you already told me that on the phone what they are?' he said testily.

'We have interviewed a witness regarding the second murder sir and she was able to provide us with a picture of the suspect.'

Grant's ears pricked up. 'So you have a picture eh, well that's wonderful we'll get it to the Press at once.'

'Begging your pardon sir, but I would rather you didn't do that.'

'Why man? it will be a golden opportunity to show that we are making progress and it may bring more witnesses forward.'

'It could also put the killer on his guard; or worse still he could just disappear and start up somewhere else sir.'

He then went on to tell the Inspector what the Pathologist had deduced from the post mortem about the killer. '

'Which brings me to my main reason for coming to see you sir' Cooper said 'In order to cover the search area efficiently I need more men.'

'Out of the question Cooper, I've already stated the position regarding manpower.'

Cooper jumped up out of his chair and put his hands on the front of Grant's desk; between gritted teeth he shouted.

'With all due respect sir, what are we running here, a bunch of superannuated boy scouts or a Crime force?'

12

'This man has already killed three girls that we know of and the evidence is that he won't stop until we catch him and all I have to solve this case is two constables and a boy' 'They are tired and demoralized, they need some support and back up from you sir.' 'If you think it is still out of the question I wish to have an interview with the Superintendent so I can tender my resignation.'
He turned on his heels and strode out of the door leaving the Inspector open mouthed.

   Later that afternoon Cooper's phone rang, he picked it up expecting to hear that he had been suspended. It was the Superintendent.
      'I hear that you are in need of more men Cooper and that you are making good progress in the murder case, how many do you need?'
Cooper couldn't believe his good fortune and thought of a number and doubled it; there was a pause at the other end of the phone and then the Super said,
      'I'll see what I can do Cooper; keep up the good work.'
In the end he got fifteen extra men and a larger room; it was good to see the improvement in his team's morale, even Whitlum was caught smiling. Soon he had teams covering the area from Yarmouth up to Norwich interviewing the occupants of boats moored up; but so far without any sign of the killer. Cooper sent Whitlum, Medler and Foley to scour the records of hirings over the last six weeks at all the boatyards in Wroxham. Unfortunately they drew a blank; no one could remember someone who looked like the photo fit. It looked as if the man had hired the boat from somewhere else; so the search was spread to all boatyards in the region. This was a colossal task as there were literally dozens dotted about the County.

Then another girl was found; but this time she was discovered in the dunes at Yarmouth North beach by a man walking his dog. Cooper sent a team over to Yarmouth to help the local Police and the search quickly switched to the moorings on the land side of the town. Medlar rang in to say that they had information regarding a cruiser with private registration moored up; but no one seemed to have seen the occupant since it arrived.

'We're going aboard now sir and I will report back.' So saying Medlar rang off.

Cooper had a bad feeling about it and endeavored to contact Medlar to hold off until he got there.

As he went down the stairs the desk sergeant shouted up to him 'phone call for you'

He picked up the phone from the desk and heard a strange voice shouting hysterically.

'The bastard has blown up the boat, it was booby trapped. Seven of our men have been killed and God knows how many bystanders are hurt.'

Through the numbness of shock he heard himself saying,

'Who is that speaking?'

'Inspector Warren, Yarmouth CID, can you get down here and give us a hand to sort out this mess?'

'I'm on my way.' shouted Cooper; throwing the phone down he raced out to his car.

CHAPTER FOUR

When he arrived at the moorings the last of the ambulances was just leaving; he parked his car and ran over to where the Inspector was waiting. The smell of diesel oil hung heavily in the air, there was also a more sickening stench of death and the concreted area where the cruiser had been was blackened and scorched. He picked his way carefully between the bits of debris and unidentifiable pieces of human flesh to look over the edge into the river. The main spars of the hull poked out of the water like despairing blackened fingers and an oil slick was floating slowly downstream.

He walked back to Inspector Warren, who was still in shock,
'How many,' asked Cooper?
'Seven dead and twelve wounded, two have lost limbs, I'm sorry about your men, and they were first on board.'
Cooper felt he was about to pass out, 'where have they been taken?'
'To the police morgue, I'll take you down there when we are finished here,' replied Warren. '
'How come there were not more boats sunk' Cooper said?
'Pure luck,' admitted Warren, 'apparently one left early this morning and the other had cast off about ten minutes before we went on board.'
They oversaw the clean up and then Cooper followed the Inspector's car to the morgue.

As he walked in and saw the bodies laid out on trestle tables anger welled up inside him. This homicidal lunatic had murdered these upholders of the law without an ounce of conscience. These dedicated men had given their all to ensure Public safety and this was their reward. He walked slowly down the line of bodies till he found what was left of Whitlum and Medlar. He reflected bitterly that they were both married with children and he dreaded having to break the news to the families.

'Come and have a drink, we could both do with one,' suggested Warren.

'No thanks I have to go and see if my Police Cadet is in the hospital.'

'All the survivors have been taken to Gorleston Infirmary Sergeant; I'll drive you down if you like.'

'That's all right I know where it is,' said Cooper slowly; 'thanks for the offer anyway, I'll be in touch.'

He walked in a daze to his car and drove towards Gorleston, arriving at the hospital without noticing a thing during the journey; his mind was a blank. He showed his ID card at reception and was directed to a ward on the second floor, it was full of people injured by the blast. He looked around and at first he could not see Foley; his heart sank, had they missed an eighth body? Then he saw an arm waving slowly at the far end of the ward; quickly he reached the bedside of the lad.

He was swathed in bandages and one leg was suspended in a cradle, 'how are you feeling Foley?' he asked.

'I've had better days Sergeant, 'they say that I'll be discharged in about a week.'

'What happened?' asked Cooper.

'Whitlum and Medlar boarded the cruiser and went into the cabin, I had just stepped on to the deck when the bomb went off; it blew me into the water and someone

16

fished me out. 'They say that's what saved me and that apart from third degree burns and a broken leg I should be ready for duty.'

Cooper felt a lump coming into his throat and turned away; the bravery of this young man was in the best tradition of the Force

'Is there anything you need Foley, just name it and I'll see you get it?'

'No sir, I just want to get back to work and help to catch this 'nutter' before he kills anyone else.'

The fourth victim of the killer was a local girl; but the way she died was the same, except she had not been found in water. Perhaps he had been disturbed before dumping the body and left the scene; one thing was certain however, he was aware that the police were closing the net and had rigged the boat to kill as many as possible. He looked at the forensic report regarding the explosion; it had the stamp of Army all over it. The plastic explosive had been attached to the gas bottles in the galley and the detonator actuated by an electric pulse triggered by a wire fixed to the cabin door. By now he could be anywhere; it was time to get the Press involved. He rang Inspector Grant and asked for a meeting with the National and local news hounds. At nine oclock next morning he met the press and handed out copies of the Photo fit picture of the killer; appealing for anyone with information to come forward or contact him personally. The phones were hot for the next week; mostly time wasters and lime lighters, but there were several possible witnesses who claimed to have seen a tall man with cropped hair and a scar He asked these people to call into the station to make statements and took them personally.

The first caller was a woman who had been going home by the moorings, she claimed that she had seen the cruiser come down river and tie up at about nine in the evening. She saw a tall man wearing a camouflaged jacket and trousers making the vessel fast, he then walked away towards the town. She also noticed that he was carrying a large military style rucksack on his back. Another witness saw a man answering to that description studying a timetable at Yarmouth station about one hour later. Cooper sent men to the station to gather any further information.

He reported to Inspector Grant and informed him of the witness's statements;

'It looks as if he has left the area' said Grant.

'I'm not so sure sir; it seems to me that he sees us as an adversary to be beaten by his superior wit and cunning.'

'It's a game to him and he is determined to win it, his ego demands it.'

'You think he will remain in Norfolk Cooper?' said Grant in surprise.'

'Yes sir I do and I think he will be contacting us in some way soon; he still has the initiative and the advantage that we don't know where he is'

Two days later Cooper had the answer, a letter arrived from the killer; it consisted of letters cut from an Eastern Daily paper. It read; 'Dear Mr. Plod, such a shame about your men; but if they will stick their noses into my little games they will pay the price and that goes for you too. I intend to play another little game on Friday so you had better get your thinking cap on,'

The Reaper.

Cooper sat holding the letter with his brain working furiously; the message was plain enough, it was a direct personal challenge to cross swords with this self styled Reaper. He sent the letter to Forensics, but as he thought there were no finger prints on it or the envelope. The letter had been posted in Thurne so he immediately dispatched a team to comb the area for further information. He rang the Ministry of Defence and asked for the department dealing with lists of Army personnel. He was put through to someone with a 'cut glass' accent and a distinctly disdainful manner. Cooper explained the situation and when he had finished there was a moment's silence at the other end of the line.

'I cannot divulge that information' was the frosty reply, 'you will have to clear it with Security.'

Cooper sighed: 'can you give me a number to ring?' he said with exaggerated politeness.

'I'm afraid not; it is classified' the stuffed shirt responded.

'For Christ's sake man this maniac has killed eleven people to date with a promise to continue killing' he shouted.' 'What would you do if war was declared; put the message in the out tray and twiddle your thumbs?' 'I want to speak to your Superior now; otherwise I can promise you that you will be looking for a job tomorrow.'

'Hello, Sir Perry Warnes here; how can I be of service? The voice on the line sounded brisk and business like.

Cooper went over the whole thing again.

I see' said Sir Perry, 'can you narrow it down a bit?'

'We think that he could be ex Special Forces and that he may have been serving in a hot country recently.'

'Right, I will get somebody on to it right away and ring you back, this man will have to be stopped.'

Cooper put down the phone and rolled himself a cigarette;

just then the phone rang, it was one of the team he had sent over to Thurne.

'I don't know whether this is relevant Sarge; but the village shop was broken into last night and a lot of canned food and other stuff was stolen.' 'The thing is the Post Master and his wife sleep over the shop and never heard a thing; it was only when he came down to do the papers that he noticed.'

'Lucky for them that they didn't' said Cooper, 'or they would be two more statistics in this damned case.'

'It's got to be our man and it would seem that he is living rough somewhere in the area, 'I'll send a squad down to help you; see if the local force will spare you some men who are familiar with the terrain.'

'Very good Sarge; shall you be coming down here yourself?'

'I'm waiting for some information about this psycho then I will,' replied Cooper and rang off.

Things were beginning to move; somehow he had to catch the Reaper off guard and a man hunt might be the way to put him on the defensive.

CHAPTER FIVE

Sir Perry was as good as his word, he rang back later in the afternoon,

'Hello, I think we've found our man, it took a lot of checking as he had been invalided out after exhibiting psychotic behavior' 'He was serving in Aden behind enemy lines in Yemen; your description seems to fit as well. 'The report and photos will reach you tomorrow morning, special delivery. 'Good luck Sergeant I hope you soon catch the blighter.'

Cooper went upstairs and knocked on the Inspector's door, entered and brought him up to date.

'Well done Cooper, that was an excellent piece of initiative" said Grant.' The atmosphere between them had seemed to improve since his outburst.

'Thank you sir, there was one other thing; I would like to have armed officers included in the hunt for this man. 'He is bound to be armed himself and has already proved how resourceful he can be.' Grant sucked his teeth, 'Firearms are always tricky Cooper; lots of things can go wrong.'

'I know sir, but I can't let unarmed officers take this guy on, it would be plain murder.'

'Hmm, point taken Cooper, but I will hold you responsible for the outcome; keep me informed.'

With that he took up some papers he had been reading and said pointedly

'Close the door on your way out will you.'

Cooper smiled wryly, 'the 'Old Man' always has to remind you he is in charge' he thought.

Next morning there was an envelope on his desk, it was the information Sir Perry had promised him. He opened it and a photo fell out with the papers; he was looking at the face of the Reaper. It was obviously an official picture as the man was in full uniform; his face was long with a prominent jaw and close set eyes. There was something terrible in those eyes, which seemed to stare like those of a predator about to kill its prey. Cooper shivered involuntarily as he picked up and read the psychiatric report. 'Illusions of invincibility and superiority, sadistic impulses, without any human feelings' The report went on and on taking up psychoanalysis, drug therapy and constant monitoring. The man's name was Robert Duffy. So why was this creature loose amongst the community? That was the million dollar question. He was still asking himself the answer to this question when he arrived outside the Black Swan in Thurne. His colleague, Sergeant Mullins was waiting for him and they went into the Snug, he ordered two pints of best bitter and they sat in a corner seat to confer. Cooper rolled a cigarette and lit it; blue smoke curling up towards the old beams.

'What have you got for me Geoff?'
Mullins sipped his bitter reflectively.

'To be honest we have'nt seen or heard anything that would help us to pinpoint where he is.' 'The locals are a pretty close bunch and if they do know anything they are keeping it to themselves.'

'He can't be far away, because tomorrow he is going to strike again,' said Cooper; 'We have to locate him or at least disrupt his plans,' that way he may start making mistakes and we will get a lead on him.'

Cooper called the landlord over and asked where they could hire a motor boat in the village; he smiled and said.

'As a matter of fact sir I have one moored in the dyke behind the pub.'

'That's great' said Cooper, 'could we hire it for a couple of hours?'

'Certainly sir, I will get the boy to show you where it is; the tank is full, but be careful she's a powerful boat and there is a speed limit on the river;' then he laughed; 'but then I shouldn't have to tell you that sir should I?'

Five minutes later they came out of Thurne Dyke into the Bure with the powerful engine burbling in low revs; Cooper turned right into the busy waterway and opened her up, weaving between the yachts and holiday cruisers.

'What are those buildings on the right bank Geoff?' 'Are they wind pumps and if so are they still in use?'

'I don't know,' said Mullins; 'we've mainly concentrated on finding a tent or some sort of hideout in the countryside round here.'

'I think we had better check them out don't you?' said Cooper trying to keep the annoyance out of his voice.

Where the river widened he turned the boat round and headed back to Thurne Dyke.

After mooring up they set off across the marshes towards the two old wind pumps; they looked very like traditional windmills except they pumped water instead of grinding flour. The Broads were dotted with them and they controlled the level of the rivers in high tides and floods. The first looked neglected and had a rusty padlock on the door; Cooper studied it carefully for signs of recent use, but there were no new scratches so he walked on to the next one.

This was more promising; the padlock on the door was new and not of the same type; looking round he fished a bunch of assorted keys from his pocket and began trying them in the lock.

'You haven't seen this Geoff have you,' he said. 'What,' said Sergeant Mullins looking the other way?

'Oh, that's lucky' said Cooper, unlocking the door, 'it was open all the time.'

They cautiously went inside; it smelt musty and damp and there were cobwebs everywhere. The machinery of the water pump took up most of the ground floor, but there was a stairway up to the top of the building where the sails turned the drive shaft. Cooper put his finger to his lips and pointed up the stairs, he began to climb and Mullins followed. Half way up one of the wooden treads squeaked loudly and Cooper winced; he drew his truncheon and Mullins did the same. Reaching the top of the stairs Cooper rushed into the room; it was empty except for the footprints of a large man in the dust; the bird had flown. Cooper was angry; not so much with Mullins for missing an obvious hiding place, but with himself for not getting down here sooner to keep an eye on things. Now they had to start all over again and time was not on their side! The radio telephone in his car was squawking as he came round to the front of the pub; he rushed over and picked up. The search team had located a one man tent inside the ruins of St. Benet's Abbey on the edge of the river upstream. The bad news was that there was no sign of the Reaper although there were tinned goods and a spirit stove inside. Cooper ordered the main body of the men to withdraw and leave a couple of armed men to keep the site under surveillance in case the killer returned. In his heart of hearts though he did not think he would, obviously the man had been watching the search team. For one thing he had taken his sleeping bag with him as well as his rucksack; that pointed to the fact that he was heading somewhere else, but where? He rang Inspector Grant and brought him up to date with the situation.

'I think there is nothing for it except a concerted search sir; we can do with every one that can be spared, this place is a watery wilderness and the man could stay undetected indefinitely.' Grant promised to do what he could; 'what about the Army Cooper?' he suggested, 'they may be able to help?'

'Thank you sir, I will follow that up immediately.' He rang off and called up Directory enquiries who gave him the number of the local Army base.

He was put through to the Adjutant who was lukewarm about the idea 'Like to help old boy; but they are mostly out on maneuvers on Thetford Battle Area d'ye see; have to keep a certain number of bods here for the security of the camp.'

Cooper thanked him and rang off; rolling himself yet another cigarette he lit up and called Mullins. He arranged for two groups to search either side of the Bure, starting from the St Benets area and moving away from the river into the marshy regions running alongside. He had put local men in each team to direct the search with specific orders to check every unoccupied building on the way. He joined the search on the Thurne side of the river and they set off in a line abreast, each man was wearing wellington boots and had a long staff to poke the undergrowth. As they moved forward startled birds burst out of the reeds in fright; Cooper grimaced, no doubt there would be repercussions from the Wildlife lobby about this operation, but the circumstances outweighed disturbing a few birds.

Despite the situation he could not help marveling at the wild beauty of these watery regions; the mystery and solitude of what was after all a man made landscape. The Broads were created by peat diggings over centuries which had eventually been flooded by the local rivers to form this dramatic landscape. As if to emphasize his thoughts a Heron flapped lazily by on its way to the next fishing spot. His reverie was broken suddenly; first he missed his footing and fell, as he did so something that sounded like an angry hornet flashed over him. There was a cry of pain from behind him and a splash as someone fell; picking himself up he turned to see two constables lifting up one of their colleagues who had a short metal arrow in his arm. They were under fire; they must be closing on the Reaper, he shouted to everyone to stop and get down; sending the armed men to try and outflank him

The noise from the river had almost ceased as the cruisers and yachts began to moor up for the night, the sun was beginning to climb down the sky its light illuminating the feathery tops of the reeds till they glowed like burnished gold. Cooper had to admit that they had lost their man; he had slipped away whilst the search party was cautiously moving forward. He called his men in and they retraced their steps back towards St Benet's Abby; their body language reflecting their disappointment and tiredness.

Before dismissing them he endeavored to raise their moral; 'Men don't be dispirited by today's lack of success; you were up against a man of great experience in survival and being elusive, however we have chased him out of two hideouts and were very nearly on the point of catching him.' Let's hope tomorrow we shall have more success and take this maniac in to custody;

now get an early night as we start again tomorrow at six am.

He turned to Mullins and asked if there was any news of the injured constable. 'He's had the arrow removed and been patched up; fortunately it went through the fleshy part of the arm so it didn't damage any muscles or tendons.' 'That arrow was meant for you Dan' he went on; 'lucky you fell at the precise moment he fired.'

'You mean bolt, not arrow; it was fired from a small crossbow' said Cooper, 'lethal up to about fifty yards.'

'Fancy a pint before turning in?' said Mullins. 'No thanks Geoff, I'm dog tired; must be getting out of condition, but to quote the Bard, 'The sleep that knits up the raveled sleeve of care; is what I need.'

He had taken a room at the Black Lion, which unfortunately was over the bar; he was kept awake till closing time by some local 'sons of rhythm' murdering popular songs. Finally he dropped off and awoke with a start as his travel clock began dinning in his ears. Hurriedly getting showered and shaved, he dressed and went out to direct the day's operations.

CHAPTER SIX

There was a mist hanging over the marshes and the rising watery sun shone blood red through the reeds. Cooper shivered; it was quite cold despite being August, he directed the men to a pile of riot shields which he had sent for the previous evening. Each man took one and they lined up ready to move off, at least the shields offered some protection against any further attacks by crossbow. At his signal the men began to move forward in line; he had also taken the precaution of sending another search team to the other side of the area of marsh they were beating. That way, hopefully, escape would be made more difficult for the fugitive if he was in this section. They had to disrupt the Reaper's plan to conduct another of his lethal games if at all possible. In two hours they had emerged from the reed beds and were confronting the team lined up at the other side. They swept three sections of marsh in this way without seeing either hair or hide of the Reaper. Cooper was beginning to worry; he lit a roll up and thought hard, it seemed the man was playing with them getting them to search the marshes while he set up his 'game' somewhere else.

He left Mullins in charge and walked back to his car, sure

enough the phone was going. Picking up, he said, 'what have you got?'

'A message from the Reaper sarge; it was dropped in our box about ten minutes ago.'

'What does it say?'' Cooper asked wearily.

'Well Sarge it's a sort of riddle,' said the constable.

'Read it to me will you?' Cooper said, fumbling for his notebook.

The man cleared his throat as if he were about to make a speech; 'I say seek and ye shall find, my work in windmills of the mind.'

'Right I've got it,' said Cooper as he finished scribbling; 'thanks for the oration, but I advise you to keep the day job,' with that he rang off. 'Windmills of the mind,' he mused; 'that can only mean one of the pump houses, probably the one we already looked in. 'He told Mullins what had happened who was all for dashing off to check it out. 'That would not be a good idea; knowing his track record he has probably left us a little present,' reflected Cooper lighting yet another roll up. 'Can you get hold of an extension ladder,' he asked?

'I'll ask around,' said Mullins and he went out; he was back in half an hour with two constables carrying the sort of ladder that builders use.

'Come on Geoff, the fewer of us the better in case we find his present.' stated Cooper.

They set out for the pump houses with the two constables carrying the ladder bringing up the rear. Arriving outside the second building Cooper had the extension ladder set high enough to reach the small window of the top floor. He hated heights; trying to refrain from looking down he climbed up to the window and looked in. It was difficult to see anything at first as the window was encrusted with years of dust; he rubbed it with his sleeve and peered in. The sight that met his eyes confirmed his worst fears; there was a naked girl trussed up and tied to one of the wooden pillars. Near her, but just out of her reach was a large lump of Semtex explosive wired to a cheap alarm clock and a battery? She was gagged; but her eyes expressed the sheer terror she was feeling. He removed his jacket and wrapped it round his arm, and then he proceeded to break the window and remove the remaining shards of glass.

He shouted down to Mullins what he had seen; 'Whatever you do don't try to come up the stairs; he is bound to have left another device somewhere about.' Carefully he grasped the window frame and put his left leg over the sill; as he did so the ladder moved slightly, he came out in a cold sweat; recovering he managed to climb into the room.

He smiled reassuringly at the girl and moved over to the bomb; first carefully removing the detonator from the Semtex. At least if that went off it would only be a small bang. He looked the mechanism over to see if there were any connections going elsewhere; but could see none; carefully unwinding the leads from the battery he rendered the bomb safe. Next he untied the girl and gave her his jacket, which didn't cover all her modesty, but at least it would restore some warmth as her skin was icy cold with shock. He moved to the door and looked down the staircase; sure enough the Reaper had booby trapped it, one of the treads had been prized up and he guessed there would be a pressure plate fitted underneath which would activate the device.

He shouted down to Mullins, 'I've defused the bomb up here, but there's another on the stairs; get the Bomb Squad here tout suit and could you send up a greatcoat

for the lady.' After the stair bomb had been rendered safe he brought the girl downstairs; she was still in extreme shock and was unable to give him any details,
'I shall have to wait until she recovers before I can interview her,' he said as she was taken away in an ambulance to the Cottage Hospital.
He seconded two men to guard her overnight in case the Reaper tried to kill her; as she must have seen him and could recognize him. He had won a small victory in foiling the Reaper's 'game', but by no means had he won the war.

CHAPTER SEVEN

Sir Peregrine, Millington, Smythe KBE; Chairman of Crown Oil laid down the Financial Times and frowned, he did not like the current situation at all. He picked up the phone and spoke to someone who eliminated awkward situations for him.

'The man is becoming a liability and may well start the authorities looking in directions that would be embarrassing for some people in high places; he needs to be removed, but not by the police, do you understand?'

There was a reply in the affirmative; 'Well see to it and let me know the outcome,' he said replacing the phone.

Pity he thought, the man was the perfect killing machine; he had certainly been admirable reversing the military coup in Abundu. Now here he was still at large and conducting a one man killing spree in the Norfolk Broads. He had always known that the man was mentally unstable; after all he had arranged for him to break out of the private psychiatric unit so that he could lead the Mercenaries paid for by Crown Oil.

Sir Peregrine had joined the company on retiring from the Army and had rapidly risen to his present position with a reputation for getting things done, one way or another. He had been instrumental in doing deals with that wily old bird Ibudongo in Abundu in order to exploit the large offshore oil deposits. Unfortunately Ibudongo reacted in the usual way of many African dictators and siphoned the oil revenues into personal Swiss bank accounts; whilst his unfortunate subjects saw none of the benefits he had promised them. Things eventually came to a head and there was a military led uprising causing Ibudongo to flee to the Arab Emirates and the military to take over the oil fields and nationalize them. Crown Oil had invested a great deal of money in exploration and development as well as large bribes to local politicians and considered that the coup was definitely not cricket. So the mercenaries landed in two old Dakotas on the airstrip outside the capital and proceeded to show the local army how efficient they were until the remainder fled into the bush.

Crown Oil technicians and rig workers moved back and the status quo was restored. The United Nations objected; but did nothing to rock the boat so Big Business had its way yet again. Now because of this 'loose cannon' things could start to unravel with unpredictable consequences.

CHAPTER EIGHT

Cooper called in at the Cottage Hospital to see if the girl had recovered sufficiently to be interviewed. He was ushered into a small annex where she was sitting up looking much better; she smiled at him as he arrived.

'How are you feeling this morning?' he said.

'Much better, thanks to you,' she replied and then she blushed, obviously remembering how much of her he had seen.

'I was hoping you could tell me something about the man who abducted you,' he said.

She looked serious then; 'he was wearing a mask when he took me,' she said, and went on to explain that she had been jogging at about seven oclock in the morning before going to work. 'He grabbed me as I ran down the path that runs through the wood near my house.'

'Was there anything about him that sticks in your mind?' asked Cooper.

'Yes the top joint of the middle finger on his left hand was missing; I noticed it as he put his hand over my mouth.'

'What sort of build was he?' said Cooper.

'Tall and muscular; he seemed very fit because he just threw me over his shoulder and ran with me across the marshes to that old windmill,' 'He tied me up and set up that bomb; then he went downstairs and I could hear him doing something there.'

'Did he speak to you at all?' Cooper asked.

'No not directly; he seemed to be speaking his thoughts out loud, I remember him saying something about windmills of the mind then he laughed; it was horrible.'

Cooper thanked her as he could see that recall of the incident was beginning to upset her.

'I'll call in again tomorrow morning to see how you are; then I expect you will want to go home.'

While he was driving back to Thurne a message came through on the car phone, it was Foley; he had been discharged from hospital and was manning the phone as his leg was still in plaster.

'How are you getting on?' said Cooper awkwardly, feeling guilty as he had not been able to get away to see the lad again in hospital.

'Glad to be back sergeant, if they had kept me in any longer I think I would have gone mad with boredom.'

'Oh, by the way, we've received a message for you from the Reaper, he seems to be annoyed.'

'Good,' said Cooper, 'what does it say?'

'He rants on about spoiling his little game and says the next clue will be much more obscure.'

'Does he mention a date?'

'Fraid not, I think you have really upset him this time; he said that you seemed to be less stupid than he thought,' replied Foley.

'Don't take liberties Foley, or you'll be back on filing,' said Cooper, 'see you soon.' He replaced the phone and grinned to himself, cheeky young bugger, he thought.

CHAPTER NINE

Nicholson checked into a Motel just off the Yarmouth Road taking his own luggage to his chalet; which consisted of a black suitcase and what looked like a bag of golf clubs. He opened the suitcase and put his clothes in the wardrobe and chest of drawers; then he picked up the golf bag and took the top section off. Inside there were a collection of weaponry including a high powered rifle complete with scope; a sawn off shotgun and several handguns. The ball pocket on the side of the case contained ammunition of various calibers and two hunting knives; it seemed he had come prepared for any or all situations. Nicholson was a nondescript looking character with a face like an unmade bed and spade like hands. He would easily merge into a crowd and be unnoticed; however he was retired S.A.S and had seen action in many theaters of conflict where British interests were concerned.

He had been charged by Millington Smythe to eliminate the problem of Duffy and he had no illusions about the magnitude of the risk involved. He had actually worked with the guy and had not liked him from the start; Duffy was a loner and would just disappear during an action, presumably to do his own thing, then return covered in blood from his killings with the blood lust still in his eyes. Yes he really enjoyed killing for its own sake; it seemed to turn him on in some way. He checked each weapon in turn oiling the working parts and cleaning each barrel with a piece of cloth on a pull through. Having satisfied himself that all was in order he selected an old World War One long barreled Luger automatic, loaded it with 9mm ammunition and slipped it into a small wash leather holster under his left arm. It was still one of the most reliable hand guns available and he had never known it to jamb. He picked up the phone and asked for an outside line; he waited till he heard the click as the receptionist put her phone down then he rang a local number.

'Hallo, is that you Graham; I want to hire your 'egg beater' tomorrow for a reconnaissance of the Broadland area, is that O.K.?' 'You had better give me directions to that hideaway of yours,' he jotted down some road numbers and then signed off, 'see you tomorrow at seven, cheerio.'

Graham Singleton was an ex Naval pilot who had converted onto helicopters at the end the war; after being caught smuggling heroin out of Hong Kong whilst his ship was stationed there; he was given a dishonorable discharge and a spell in jail. However he had sufficient funds to purchase an old Sikorski S.51Dragonfly and now made reasonable living flying businessmen around the UK. He had done work for Nicholson before so therefore he asked no questions as he ran up the engine, checked the flying controls, then engaging the collective he climbed up to one hundred feet before moving off towards the Broads.

Nicholson sat in the left hand seat with a pair of powerful binoculars on his lap; thanks to the large perspex canopy he had an uninterrupted view of the terrain as they flew low towards their goal. He slipped the Luger out of the holster;

37

removed the clip and checked it, then returned it to the holster.

Singleton shouted above the noise of the engine, 'I didn't realize you would be armed; I don't like firearms aboard my 'chopper,' what if we have an emergency landing and the authorities get involved? I would lose my license.'

Nicholson grinned and leaning across he shouted,

'it never bothered you before Graham, you must be getting old; stop worrying I'm paying you plenty for this trip anyhow.'

They were now coming into the Broadland region and the river Bure snaked across the countryside like a huge silver python below them. The wakes of dozens of holiday craft broke the surface up into sparkling points of light as they made their way to their different destinations. Either side of the river there were great swathes of marshland carpeted with reed beds and sedges; then grazing meadows full of cattle being fattened up for market. Nicholson was not however in the least interested in the view; he had his binoculars to his eyes sweeping the land as they went looking for any sign to suggest that Duffy was in the area.

'Can you get any lower Graham?' he shouted, 'it would be helpful as I can't see much detail from here.'

The helicopter tilted and lost about fifty feet, 'This is as far as I dare go,' responded Singleton, 'otherwise some interfering busybody will report me.'

Nicholson nodded and continued to sweep the ground as they sped down the river at eighty knots.

They were soon approaching the area where Thurne Dyke joined the Bure; the last reports of the Reaper had been in this region. Nicholson swept his arm around and Singleton threw the machine into a banking turn to survey the terrain below them. A frightened flock of Mallards nearly flew into the path of the helicopter and Singleton had to take evasive action to avoid them.

'This is too risky Steve,' he said, 'I shall have to gain altitude if we are going to continue.'

Nicholson shrugged his shoulders philosophically and put the binoculars up to his eyes again. They spent about half an hour sweeping the surrounding country side without seeing any sign of their quarry and finally Singleton indicated that he was getting low on fuel. On the return journey Nicholson reflected on the size of the task he had been given; not only was he up against one of the most skilled and dangerous men he had ever encountered, but was now aware of the difficulty of finding him in this great wilderness. He would have to await the Reaper's next strike in order to pinpoint the search area; trouble was that the police would be swarming all over the place as well. He had to devise some sort of cover to justify his presence in the region; being a resourceful person there were already the stirrings of an idea formulating in his mind. As things turned out he did not have to wait long.

CHAPTER TEN

Cooper watched as the body was lifted out of the boat and laid on the bank; he felt sick as he approached and knelt down to examine what had been a young girl, full of life and vitality and now just another statistic in this deranged beast's killing spree. It was made worse by the fact that the Reaper had sent another of his notes warning of the forthcoming event. He had boasted that the clue would be more difficult to crack and the fact was that Cooper had failed to interpret it in time. It was a bitter pill to swallow and Cooper was beginning to lose heart; Forensics arrived and began their examination of the body.

He stood up and asked, 'usual 'M.O.?'

'Looks like it,' responded the Pathologist, 'no signs of a struggle, marks around the neck in the carotid region.'

Cooper walked slowly back to his car rolling up another cigarette; he put it in his mouth, but omitted to light it.

'The way things are going it won't be long before Grant will call in Scotland Yard; if only to cover himself,' he reflected.

He couldn't blame him; apart from causing Duffy some inconvenience, his own track record in this instance was abysmal.

The man had retained the initiative throughout the whole case so far; and again at this point Cooper still had no idea where he was. This girl had been pulled out of the river Thurne near Martham by local officers in response to reports of a body being seen in the water by passing craft. He stopped in Ludham on the way back for a drink; sitting in one of the high back settles in the old Georgian pub with a pint of bitter in front of him he tried to assess where he had gone wrong. He had to admit this was a unique crime for a country copper; his track record for clearing up the sort he was used to dealing with was exemplary, but this was perhaps a case too far. There had to be a break through soon; the man had to make a mistake, perhaps through over confidence he would become careless? Cooper finished his pint and returned the glass to the bar, then lighting up another 'roll up' he went out to his car.

Foley looked up as Cooper walked into the office.
'There has been a possible sighting of the Reaper Sergeant.'
'Where?' asked Cooper
'In Martham apparently,' said Foley, 'this old bloke claims to have seen him in the High Street yesterday.'
Cooper brightened up, 'has he been interviewed?'
'Only by the local force; they don't seem too impressed by his evidence as he apparently sees flying saucers over Martham quite regularly.'
Cooper groaned would his luck ever change; this old guy sounded as if he was away with the fairies.
However he couldn't afford to leave any stone unturned, so he rang the local Police Station in Martham and obtained the man's address as he did not have a phone.

He drove out and located the house; which was in a Victorian terrace just off the main street. An air of neglect and the aroma of cats hung around the dwellings as he walked up to the front door and knocked. After what seemed an age there was the sound of slow footsteps approaching and the door was opened a few inches and a face peered suspiciously at Cooper.

'You can just clear orf, I ain't voting for you lot; you ain't never done nothing for the likes of me ever.'

Cooper grinned and showed the man his I.D; there was a long pause as he screwed up his eyes and mouthed the words on the card.

'I've already told them lot down the station what I saw, and a fat lot of good it did me; I always try to be helpful and what do I get for it.'

'I would like to hear what you saw,' said Cooper; 'I have been trying to catch this man for some time.'

'Oh, well I suppose you'd better come in then,' the old man led the way down the hall which smelt of damp and stale food.

He ushered Cooper into the living room and waved him towards a misshapen settee, there was a plate with the remains of a meal on the table and a black 'moggy' regarded him with baleful eyes from the window sill.

'Would yer like a cup of tea?' the old man asked. Cooper said yes with some misgivings; but anything to help establish a rapport he thought.

The old man shuffled off and Cooper heard the sound of the kettle being filled and eventually the man returned bearing two large cups and saucers, managing to spill some tea on the way in. Finally he sat down facing Cooper and slurped some tea noisily; setting down the cup he wiped his mouth with the back of his hand and leaned forward confidentially.

'Well it were like this 'ere, I'd just gone down to the corner shop to get me milk and a paper when this tall bloke brushed past me goin' in the other direction..'

'Did you get a good look at him?' asked Cooper.

"Oh yeah, I stopped and turned round 'cos I saw that there 'photo kit' thing on the telly; as I did he turned before crossing the road and I saw the scar on his left cheek.'

Cooper said, 'did you notice what he was wearing?'

The man thought for a moment and said, 'Yeah, it were one of them camouflage army outfits; like what they wear in combat.'

Cooper pricked up his ears; that had not been disclosed on television; this man had definitely seen Duffy; 'Where do you think he could have been making for?'

'Well, he were on the road to Somerton, so I s'pose that could ha' been where he wuz a goin'.'

CHAPTER ELEVEN

Nicholson sat in his car near Thurne Dyke watching the police hurriedly packing their kit and boarding a fleet of vehicles. They were obviously on to something and he intended to follow them to wherever they were heading. He hung well back as the convoy rolled along the narrow country roads towards Martham, where the vehicles pulled up outside the Police Station. Nicholson drove past and turned into a side street, locking his car he sauntered back towards the main street to watch further developments; just then car pulled up and a plain clothes policeman got out and walked over to the disembarking search party. This had to be the man in charge; sure enough a police sergeant met him and they were immediately engaged in animated conversation.

Nicholson removed what looked like a small wireless aerial from his pocket and pointed it towards the two men. He was also wearing an earpiece from what looked like a hearing aid clipped to his shirt inside his coat. He had acquired this gadget from a contact in the CIA and it had proved most useful in eavesdropping on distant conversations.

....'definitely saw him; I know because he mentioned the camouflage outfit that Duffy was wearing and that was not mentioned in our press release.'

Nicholson pricked up his ears as he caught these words from Cooper; so that's it, Duffy had been spotted in this sleepy hamlet. He hurriedly pocketed the listening device and walked back to his car; opening the boot he slipped off his shoes and pulled on a pair of green waders. Then he shrugged on a plastic 'Mac' and waterproof cap; now he looked like your average fishing enthusiast. He had a large fishing bag, keep net, landing net and wicker fishing stool to complete the disguise. The bag contained the high powered rifle and scope as well as assorted fishing rods; whilst the steel tipped ammunition was concealed in the stool. He was ready to find and remove Millington Smythe's problem.

The police search party moved out of Martham heading in the direction of Somerton being discreetly shadowed by Nicholson. They stopped outside the village and deployed across the marsh on the left hand side of the road, spreading out in line and moving towards four wind pumps bordering the river. Nicholson carried on into the village parking in the yard of the local pub; he was now ahead of the slowly moving man hunt. Obviously the police were heading towards those windmills; so logic dictated that Duffy was probably holed up in one of them. He collected his fishing gear and walked down the loke at the side of the pub; which took him alongside the Hundred Stream. On the opposite bank were the four wind pumps, he pulled the rifle out of the bag and screwed on the silencer. Putting it back in the bag he set up a rod; cast out into the river and sat down to wait.

Cooper moved forward through the breast high reeds in line with the rest of the search party feeling an excitement that he had seldom felt during this case; now he had the advantage of surprise. They reached the first of the wind pumps and he checked the door whilst the armed officers surrounded the building. There was no evidence that the lock had been tampered with or signs that it had been entered, so he signaled to his men to move to the next one. Again there was no sign of entry; as they were approaching the third something made him look in the direction of the last wind pump. There was someone running away through the reeds; he shouted to the group and pointed towards the fleeing man, and then suddenly the man flung up his arms and disappeared. Cooper urged his men forward towards where the man had fallen; when they located him it was indeed Duffy shot neatly through the head. Cooper knew that none of his armed officers had fired their weapons, so who the hell had? This looked like a professional killing; a head shot like that whilst the man was running was almost miraculous. The bullet had exited through the back of the skull so Cooper gauged the direction the bullet had come from, but there was no sign of a living soul.

CHAPTER TWELVE

Nicholson packed his fishing gear carefully back into the boot of the car; changed from his waders into his shoes, got into the car and drove north along the Coast Road humming tunelessly. He was in a very good mood; this would earn him a bonus on top of the fee he had already received. Life was good; it had been surprisingly easy in the end, mind you it had been one of the best shots he had ever made on a moving target. He put his foot down and picked up speed; he would be changing cars in Kings Lynn and this one would be crushed; his cup of happiness was full. So full that as he swept round the next bend at sixty he had no time to avoid the petrol tanker that was coming out of a side road. There was a gigantic explosion and a ball of flame engulfed both vehicles turning them into funeral pyres for both drivers.

It was still burning when the fire engines arrived and the vehicles had been reduced to a tangle of twisted metal. There was also danger from exploding ammunition and the fire crews had to wait for the fire to subside before approaching it. Both bodies were so badly burned that they were unrecognizable so Mr. Merryweather had to rely on obtaining matching dental records to identify them. Little of any use was left of the contents in the boot of the car apart from the breech section of a rifle and that was barely recognizable due to the distortion caused by the intense heat.

He decided to advise Cooper in the light of the Reaper having been shot by person or persons unknown.

'Hello Dan, I have some evidence here that may help with the death of Duffy;' he went on to describe the remains of the rifle.

Cooper sounded exhausted; 'Thanks Gordon, I'll try and get over tomorrow; I have been tying up loose ends of this case all day and I'm heading off for an early night, thanks for the info.'

He drove back to his flat and let himself in; it wasn't much of a place, but then since his wife had left him there seemed no point in keeping up the house as he was seldom there. The place was sparsely furnished and had a neglected air about it; but it was somewhere to lay his head at the end of the day.

He rolled a cigarette and lit it while he put the kettle on; made himself a cup of coffee and settled down to unwind. Several unanswered questions kept nagging at him; who had shot Duffy and why? What was the man involved in to attract that sort of attention and the other question that he had asked at the start; how had he been allowed to freely move about in the community? The psychiatrist's report had clearly stated that he was to be kept under constant surveillance. If he had escaped from somewhere why had it not been reported? There had to be someone with great power and resources behind all this; either the Security Services or Big Business. Perhaps he could glean some information from the remains of that crash which happened shortly after Duffy was shot and only twelve miles away from the scene. He awoke with a start smelling burning; looking down he saw the remains of his cigarette had burned a hole in the rug; damn!

CHAPTER THIRTEEN

Millington Smythe was worried; he had not heard from Nicholson for two days and that was unusual; the fellow was very reliable and reported in each day as a rule. The Press was full of the shooting of the Reaper and the tabloids had a field day with the fact that the police denied having killed him. All sorts of conspiracy theories were being put forward as to why there was a blackout on the details of the case; all the police would say was that inquiries were ongoing. What sort of inquiries he wondered; why doesn't he ring; he had tried to contact Nicholson on numerous occasions, but there was no reply.

His secretary arrived with the mail and laid it on his desk, smiled and left the room. He picked up his silver letter knife and started to open the letters; just then the phone rang, it was the Managing Director, Sir Arthur Bowker.

'Look here Millington Smythe what's going on about this Reaper feller; several of our major share holders are getting jittery about the lack of closure on this business.'

'I want reassurance from you that there are no loose ends still untied; the Press are starting to ask awkward questions; get on to it straight away and get back to me personally when you've got the answers.'

Just as he was about to reply the M.D. rang off and Millington Smythe was left with his mouth open literally speechless. 'He had not been spoken to in such a manner since joining the Board.

A surge of something akin to panic gripped his being; he was going to be made the scapegoat if things started to go pear shaped and it was beginning to look as if they had.

He picked up the phone and dialed a number; 'is that the Rialto Enquiry Agency?' 'I would like to speak to Reagan; what's that? Well get him to ring this number as soon as he gets back; it's most important,' he gave the girl the number and rang off. He took out his handkerchief and mopped his brow; he noticed that his hands were shaking and said to himself, 'steady man you've been in worse situations, pull yourself together.

'To take his mind off things he continued to open his mail; mostly routine business letters, except one. It was a large manila envelope addressed to him by name; he opened it slowly with rising apprehension and removed the papers inside. It was from Nicholson and the opening statement was; 'Dear sir, you are in receipt of this letter because I am dead.' The letter fell to the desk from the nerveless fingers of the Chairman of Crown Oil.

CHAPTER FOURTEEN

It was late when Cooper finally surfaced from a deep dreamless sleep; he looked at the bedside clock, hurriedly completed his ablutions and got dressed. As he was leaving the phone started to ring, ignoring it he got into his car and backed out of the parking bay. On arrival he found a hastily written note from Foley informing him that he was required in Inspector Grant's office' as soon as he put in an appearance. He stubbed out the first cigarette of the day and went out of the door; arriving at Grant's office he knocked and went in.

'Ah, Cooper, glad you could make it,' said Grant without the slightest hint of sarcasm; 'we have had some unexpected news regarding the occupant of the car that hit the tanker.'

'Oh, what is it sir?' said Cooper slightly wary of Grant's bonhomie.

'A letter from a firm of solicitors that represented a certain Stephen Nicholson, apparently they were instructed that in the event of him not contacting them every two days they were to notify certain people including the police.' He went on; 'I must say it seems a very odd way to conduct one's self; why did he find it necessary to do such a thing?'

Probably because he was working in a dangerous area for people he didn't trust;' said Cooper.' It's not unknown in the Underworld and also with people who work for the Security Services. 'May I see the letter sir?'
Grant handed it over and Cooper noted the name and address of the solicitors; it was couched in strictly legal terms and gave no other information regarding the deceased, apart from the fact that Nicholson ran a Security company in London.

'I would like to follow up this lead sir,' said Cooper.

Grant's eyes widened, 'why Sergeant, you have completed this case as far as your jurisdiction goes; I shall be referring this evidence to the Met,' it's their 'baby' now.'

Cooper saw red; rising from his chair he spoke with suppressed anger in his voice,

'Look sir these events happened on my turf; my team and I worked our fingers to the bone to stop this maniac; only for this Nicholson guy to come along and shoot him through the head.' 'That is an unlawful killing in my book and to simply hand it over to another force is spitting in the faces of those officers who gave their lives to apprehend him; at least allow me to work with the Met.' on this one.'

Grant's mouth tightened, 'I think you could do with a holiday Cooper; obviously the strain of it all has proved too much, consider yourself on two weeks leave from today, hopefully you will come back refreshed and more reasonable; close the door on your way out.'

Cooper stormed out and slammed the door; he was seething with rage, that pompous ass had obviously bided his time to get his own back.

As things turned out he never got that holiday; the Superintendent had the same feelings about the case as Cooper and had insisted that as the assassination of Duffy had occurred Norfolk there would be no transfer to the Met; but instead asked for their co-operation.

'As this is a joint operation Cooper you will report directly to me,' the 'Super' smiled; 'we don't want any more misunderstandings do we?'

'Cooper grinned, 'Indeed not Sir,'

'You will be meeting your opposite number tomorrow; a Sergeant Munroe; very experienced I understand.'

Cooper left the 'Super's' office feeling elated; what a turn up for the book, obviously the man had gone out of his way to overrule Grant's spiteful denial of Cooper following his rightful pursuit of the case. He wondered what Munroe would be like; overbearing and keen to show these country coppers how it's done, or keen to join in solving this enigmatic case. Things between Grant and himself would now have gone from bad to worse; he would have to watch his back as he knew how vindictive Grant could be. Next morning he was summoned to the 'Super's' office where he was introduced to Alexander Munroe; an angular middle aged Scot with a neatly clipped moustache and a reserved manner. Cooper extended his hand and Munroe examined it carefully before responding, it was like shaking hands with a dead fish. Cooper's heart sank; he could already see there would be trouble ahead.

'I'm sure you will get on well together,' boomed the 'Super;' 'Sergeant Cooper is one of my best detectives and you come highly recommended Munroe; so I am sure you will both bring a swift resolution to this case.'

Munroe sniffed and studied the ceiling; 'Ahm sure that with the methods and diligence that I can bring to bear we will soon have it solved sir.'

As they left Cooper said to Munroe; 'I thought you might like to meet my team, I know they are all looking forward to it.'

Munroe looked as if he had just discovered an offensive object under his nose; 'Ah'm afraid I will no have time as I like to familiarize myself with the case notes before starting, you will find it a very useful method for the future.'

With that parting shot he swept importantly down the corridor; leaving Cooper wondering how he was going to co-operate with this self opinionated Jock.

Cooper obtained permission to visit Nicholson's solicitors and caught the train to Liverpool Street. Hailing a cab he gave the driver the address marveling at the skill of the cabby as he weaved through the congested traffic in Clerkenwell Road and turned into Harrington Road. The cab pulled up outside a row of offices;

'Here you are guv' it's the third office along.' Cooper paid the cabbie and gave him a generous tip.

'Look could you come back for me in an hour;' he said, 'I'll make it worth your while.

'Happy to,' said the driver, 'see you later;' he pulled out into the traffic and was gone. Cooper walked along to the office indicated by the driver and looked at the brass plaque on the wall, Fisher and Hornbeam, Solicitors and Commissioners for Oaths. He smiled, that latter service had always amused him; he had visions of clients standing with hand raised and all sorts of bad language issuing from their lips. Pushing open the door he walked into a narrow hallway where a golden arrow on the wall invited him to climb the steep staircase to the next floor. He arrived at the top and walked down another corridor covered in worn linoleum, the second door bore the same legend as the brass plate, but in frosted glass. He went in; there was an elderly woman pounding an Imperial typewriter as though she bore it a grudge.

She stopped and looked at him and said, 'can I help you?'

'Yes, I hope so,' said Cooper showing her his ID card; 'I am making enquiries in an ongoing case and I have reason to believe that the Firm may be able to help me.'

'Could I speak with one of the Principals regarding the matter?'

The woman was hesitant; 'have you an appointment Mr'…?

'Detective sergeant Cooper,' he said; 'and no I haven't an appointment; this is police business and I would appreciate some co-operation.'

At this she became flustered. 'Oh dear I don't know what Mr. Hornbeam would say.'

'Cooper became impatient; 'why don't you just ask him?'

Just then the door in the partition behind the front office opened and a portly gent in a pin striped suit peered out.

'Show the gentleman into my office Jasmine,'

Cooper could hardly restrain a chuckle; 'Jasmine? It was about the most inappropriate name her parents could have given her. He walked into Matthew Hornbeam's office just in time to see him shoveling papers into a desk drawer.

Hornbeam looked up and gave a guilty smile, 'Ah, just tidying up my desk sergeant; it is surprising how the paperwork mounts up.'

He ran his finger round the inside of his collar; 'Ah, how can I be of service to our esteemed representative of the

Law?' He indicated a chair and Cooper sat down; 'I have come to make enquiries about Stephen Nicholson deceased.'

Hornbeam looked relieved and guilty at the same time; 'Oh I see, well there's not much to tell really, we didn't have much contact with him I'm afraid.'

'You do have details of his business; it was mentioned in the letter you sent us,' said Cooper

'Ah, I suppose we do,' said Hornbeam doubtfully, 'but it was more of a watching brief you see.'

'What do you mean?'

'Well we had an arrangement that he would phone us every two days and instructions to dispatch certain letters to various people if he did not.

'Have you got the address of his business?'

'Er; well that information is confidential;' he said evasively.

Cooper stood up; 'it won't take me long to obtain a search warrant and charge you with obstructing a murder investigation; is that what you want?'

By now Hornbeam was beginning to sweat; without another word he tottered over to a filing cabinet and removed a thin file which he handed to Cooper.

'Thank you,' said Cooper sarcastically; he opened the file and noted the address of Nicholson Security Service Ltd. which was located in Islington just off the Balls Pond Road.' He glanced at his watch; the cabby should be back in about fifteen minutes, as he stood up Hornbeam said rather plaintively, 'Do you think I could have a receipt for the file?'

The taxi driver was as good as his word and Cooper gave him the address in Islington as they pulled out into the traffic.

56

When they arrived outside Nicholson's office Cooper was struck by the run down appearance of the place; the exterior was badly in need of a coat of paint and the windows were grimy. He rang the bell, but there was no response; going to the news agent's next door he bought some tobacco and quizzed the shopkeeper.

The man was quite helpful and obviously liked to gossip; 'Mr. Nicholson comes in here occasionally for a paper; but he seems to spend most of his time away from his office, probably touting for business.'

'Did he employ any staff?' inquired Cooper.

'Not that I ever saw; although people would come to his office sometimes, but not very often.'

'Can you tell me who the Letting Agents are for these businesses?' asked Cooper.

'Yes I'll write it down for you;' he went into the back of the shop and on returning handed Cooper a slip of paper.

They are just down the road from here; you can't miss it,' he said.

Cooper thanked him and went back to the waiting taxi, 'can you take me to this address?' he said showing the driver the slip.

They pulled up outside a prosperous looking shop front with a large sign above with the words 'Cohen Bros. Agents for Business Lettings.' He went in and was greeted by a rather showy blonde with a bust that looked in danger of doing just that. 'What can I do for you sir,' she said,' showing a large range of immaculately white teeth.

He smothered the impulse to tell her and asked to see Mr. Cohen. She minced away to a door at the back of the office, knocked and had a muttered conversation with the occupant.

She came back and treated Cooper to another of those brilliant smiles; 'Mr. Cohen will see you now sir,' she lifted the flap on the counter and allowed Cooper through, managing to brush against him as he did so.
Slightly shaken Cooper went into Cohen's office where he was greeted with a vigorous handshake.

Abraham Cohen was a distinguished looking man; immaculately dressed in a business suit with a carnation in his buttonhole.
'Take a seat sir and tell me how I can help you;' he said with a smile that outdid his receptionist's.
However, when Cooper showed him his ID the smile disappeared instantly; 'what do you want; we are a law abiding business of forty years standing.'
Cooper held up his hand, 'hold your horses Mr. Cohen; I've come to ask your help in an inquiry that I am making with regard to one of your clients.'
Cohen looked relieved and the smile returned, 'Oh I see; well we are always glad to help the police.'
His eyes however were wary and kept darting towards the door as if he were considering making a dash for it.
'I wondered if you would object to me having a look round Nicholson's Security offices,' said Cooper; 'the owner has died in tragic circumstances and we are trying to trace any relatives?'
Cohen looked concerned; 'you mean he won't be renting the premises any more?'
'Not unless he returns from the dead,' said Cooper laconically.
Cohen stood up; 'I'll get you the keys,' he said resignedly, 'you will return them when you've finished as they are the only other set.'

Cooper took the keys and thanked him for his co-operation and ran the gauntlet of the receptionist's attentions on the way out.

Returning to Nicholson's premises he let himself in, noticing the mail scattered over the floor; he picked his way through it and went into the main office. He stopped in his tracks, the place had been ransacked; all the drawers in the filing cabinets were hanging out and there were files all over the floor Someone had been looking for something specific, but what? He went over to the desk and had a cursory look through what paperwork there was; as he did so he noticed that one of the drawers was locked. He picked up a steel paper knife from the desk and proceeded to pick the lock, eventually managing to force it open. Whoever had been searching had missed this one; perhaps they were short of time or had been disturbed by someone and in their haste had overlooked it? He took out the contents and laid them on the desk, they were mainly receipts and bank statements. He looked through the statements and whistled to himself as he saw some of the entries. This man was receiving large amounts of money from various clients, including big companies. So why was the place so down at heel; or was it just a front for something else? He gathered the bank statements together and put them in the pocket of his raincoat; then he took out his handkerchief, picked up the phone and dialed Whitehall 1212.

CHAPTER FIFTEEN

The taxi ran him back to Liverpool Street just in time to catch the five fifteen to Norwich; it was a corridor train so he availed himself of the buffet and had a couple of beers. I think I've earned them, he thought, what he had found in Nicholson's office was going to lead them to whoever was behind this case. Norwich station clock showed seven thirty two as he walked to his car; he drove straight back to his flat and spent the rest of the evening studying the entries in the bank statements. One firm's name kept coming up time and again, Crown Oil. There was something niggling at the back of his mind regarding this company; weren't they involved in something dodgy in Africa? He yawned and looked at his watch; eleven thirty he decided to call it a day and to trawl through the back issues of the dailies at the Library tomorrow.

Next morning he was summoned to the Superintendent's office; as he entered he noticed that Munro was standing by the side of the 'Super's desk.

'Morning Cooper,' said Trafford looking grim; 'Sergeant Munroe has brought a serious matter to my attention regarding the sharing of information between you; he claims you went to London yesterday and during your investigations removed information of a sensitive nature from the offices of Nicholson without permission.'

Munroe looked smug and self righteous; Cooper looked him in the eye and unzipped the brief case he was carrying.

Putting the documents that he had collected on the 'Super's desk, he said calmly, 'when I entered the office yesterday it was with keys supplied by the letting agent; someone had already ransacked the place, but had missed a locked drawer in Nicholson's desk.' 'I also left a message at the Met advising them of what I had done; that is probably where the Sergeant got his mistaken information.'

Trafford wheeled round and looked at Munroe, 'I think that you owe Sergeant Cooper an apology; it is obvious that he acted in good faith.'

Munroe's face was a picture; all his self righteousness disappeared as he tried to extricate himself from the mess of his own making.

Trafford dismissed him, saying that he would have a word with him later; turning to Cooper he said, 'give me a résumé of what you have discovered.'

He listened intently as Cooper explained the significance of the bank statements and other documents he had found..

'This is most important material, what do you propose to do now Cooper?'

'Go to the Library sir to look through the newspapers; I have a feeling that there is a link of some kind with Crown Oil.'

Trafford frowned, 'be careful Cooper you are dealing with very powerful people; we can't afford to lock horns with them without conclusive evidence.'

'I appreciate that sir; I just want to get to the truth of this case if only for the sake of my men who lost their lives and the families of the murdered girls.'

'Most commendable Cooper; but keep me in the picture at all times,' he picked up the phone and dismissed Cooper with a wave of his hand.

Cooper waded through the back issues of the Dailies until he came to 1959; there he found what he had been looking for.

The headline screamed 'Oil Company gets own back;' the column going on to describe how mercenaries retook the oilfields in Abundu. The papers were full of it; some with lurid details of the casualties inflicted on the local army; others outraged at the action; complaining of the lack of will at the United Nations to take punitive measures against Crown Oil for unlawful aggression against a Third World country. One even had an article written in defense of the action by the chairman of the Company; a certain Millington Smythe. There was a picture of him which Cooper homed in on; it showed a strong faced individual with a military bearing and a ruthless expression. Cooper was pretty sure the he was looking at the man who was responsible for the chain of events that had enabled Duffy to carry out his killing spree in Norfolk. Happy with the evidence he had found he drove back to the station and found Foley still going through the other documents he had found in Nicholson desk as well as the file he had obtained from Hornbeam.

'Anything interesting turned up Foley?' he asked.

'As a matter of fact there is; did you know Nicholson had a daughter?'

'Did he now,' exclaimed Cooper excitedly; 'well done lad; is there an address by any chance?'

'Yes and a phone number.'

'Splendid, let's have a look;' Foley handed him the file.
Apparently Sheila Nicholson lived in Swindon and
worked as a teacher in a Primary school.

He rang her that evening and introduced himself; she had
already been informed of her father's death by Hornbeam; so
Cooper made an appointment to call over and see her the
following day. It was a long drive from Norfolk and Cooper
was quite tired by the time he found her address in a block of
flats on the outskirts of the town. He walked up two flights
of stairs and rang the doorbell; a young woman opened the
door. She was rather a severe looking person with auburn hair
scraped back into a bun; heavy rimmed spectacles and an
extremely slim figure; not his idea of a teacher in charge of
small kids. He showed her his ID card and she opened the
door wide to let him in; the flat was decorated and furnished
in the Swedish minimalist style and painted white all
throughout.

He saw a picture of a man in his middle age on the
sideboard; 'is this your dad?' he inquired.
She nodded and Cooper thought he saw a tear well up in
her eyes; 'you were close then?' he said.
'Not particularly,' she said; 'but then I saw very little of
him when he was in the Army.'
'What about when he was 'demobbed' and set up his
business in London,' asked Cooper?
'That was the strange thing,' she said; 'he seemed to spend
as much time away from home as when he was a soldier.'
'What about your mother; did she find it difficult?'
She grimaced, 'mum left us when we were abroad in
Singapore for another sergeant. I don't hear from her
now.'
"How did your dad react?'

'The way men usually do; getting drunk every evening at the sergeant's mess and being grumpy during the day.'
'Who looked after you when your mother left?' he said.
'We had a Chinese maid who took care of me; she took me to school and looked after the quarters.'

She looked at him and said; 'you look tired, would you like a cup of coffee; I usually make one for myself about now.'
He thanked her and she went into the kitchen and put the kettle on; he called through;
'Did your dad talk to you about the business at all?'
'Not much,' she said, 'he was close lipped about most subjects though, probably his Army training.'
She brought the coffee through and Cooper sipped it speculatively, thank God it wasn't instant. He glanced at his watch; it was ten thirty and he was feeling too tired to drive back to Norwich.
'Is there a good Commercial Hotel near here?' he asked.
She gave him directions and he stood up; 'Thank you for seeing me, I'll leave you my card in case you think of anything that might help to clear up this case.'
He bade her goodnight and walked reflectively downstairs; she obviously didn't know much at all about her father's business or indeed anything about him. Small wonder she had grown up in the way she had, without the affection and security of a normal family life.

CHAPTER SIXTEEN

Reagan shuffled uncomfortably; Millington Smythe was giving him a tongue lashing, 'you were told to collect and bring to me all Nicholson's documents, why did you not find his bank statements?'

'There's a regular police patrol in that area and I had to be out before they came round again,' replied the unhappy gumshoe.

'Thanks to your incompetence those documents are most likely in the hands of the police and it won't take a genius to connect Nicholson with Crown Oil.'

'Fortunately we have a contact in the Force who will endeavor to lead the investigation in another direction; you had better hope that he is successful otherwise you will be joining Nicholson; now get out of my sight.'

As the unfortunate Reagan left his office Millington Smythe picked up the telephone and asked for an outside line.

He spoke at length to someone finishing with, 'I think it is about time this Cooper fellow was taken off the case; he is getting too close for comfort and it will be your head as well as mine that will roll; see to it.'

With that he rang off; opening a drawer he took out the letter that he had been sent informing him of Nicholson's death.

There was the matter of Nicholson's daughter to consider; did she pose a threat, how much did she know of her fathers affairs? The letter demanded that any monies owed to Nicholson were to be sent to her forthwith as his only next of kin. Millington Smythe grimaced; her father had been promised a bonus if he succeeded in eliminating Duffy, it seemed a shame that the Company should have to pay such a large sum to her; apart from that she was bound to question what it was for, depending on what she knew. Yes; she would have to be dealt with and the sooner the better; there had been too many slip ups already. Time was of the essence in this matter as Bowker had been ringing him every day to find out what progress was being made and Crown Oil's shares had begun to slip. He picked up the phone and began to dial.

CHAPTER SEVENTEEN

Cooper stubbed out his fourth cigarette of the morning; he had seemingly run into a wall of silence. He was being given the run around by officials of Crown Oil and their bankers; it was the 'Old Boys Network' closing ranks. He couldn't obtain a search warrant on the evidence he had and they knew it; he had to find another way. Munroe wasn't helping, constantly being uncooperative and bloody minded; determinedly plowing his own furrow and keeping whatever evidence he had found to himself.

The phone rang; it was Sheila Nicholson, 'is that sergeant Cooper?'

She sounded worried, 'how can I help you Miss Nicholson?' he responded.

"Well, I know this probably sounds paranoid; but I think I am being watched.'

Alarm bells started sounding in Cooper's head; 'Tell me about it please Miss Nicholson.'

'Please call me Sheila,' she said, 'I first noticed this dark colored car just parked up outside the school; it seemed to be there every time I arrived and left school.' 'I know most of the cars that belong to the parents; but I have never seen this one before.'

'Did you get a look at the driver?' said Cooper.

'That's the thing that made me suspicious; because every time I got near the car the driver either bent down as if to pick something up, or he turned his head away so I couldn't see his face.'

'It may be something or nothing Sheila; but to be on the safe side I'll ask the Met to send someone round to keep an eye on things.'

He tried to keep his voice light so as not to alarm her; but inside he was worried, this could be just surveillance by whoever had Duffy removed or something more sinister; either way action had to be taken.

'Just keep to your usual routine and don't go in to isolated areas; keep where there are plenty of people about, that way you shouldn't be troubled.'

She sounded relieved and after thanking him she rang off. He phoned through to the 'Met.' and advised them of the situation and asked for a surveillance team to keep an eye on Sheila. To his dismay they declined saying that they didn't have sufficient manpower available and the threat was too vague to justify such a course of action. He blew his top at this response; 'don't you people realize that she is the daughter of the 'Hit Man' and whoever hired him is probably wondering just how much she knows?' Despite his protestations they would not be persuaded and he slammed the phone down and sat fuming at their attitude. He rang Superintendent Trafford and explained the situation; the 'Super' was sympathetic; but adamant that no one could be spared from the Norfolk police either. Cooper put the phone down and tried to think of an alternative way of keeping her safe.

CHAPTER EIGHTEEN

Reagan sat in his car just down the street watching the block of flats where Sheila Nicholson lived. He didn't like this assignment one little bit; he felt like a pimp; plotting her movements for whatever reason Millington Smythe had in mind. He was more used to dealing with divorce cases or missing persons than a potential hit; but his client had put the 'frighteners' on him and he knew that you didn't refuse Crown Oil. He was an insignificant little man wearing horn rimmed glasses through which he peered myopically at the world; a mackintosh, which he wore winter and summer and his rubber soled shoes were well worn at the heels. He chewed morosely on a cheap pork pie whilst he occasionally peered through a pair of powerful binoculars at the window of her flat. The curtains were drawn and the light was on; but there was no sign of movement within; he had seen her arrive about five o'clock, but she had so far not ventured out. This was odd because normally the girl went to Yoga classes on a Monday night or rather she had done so for the last two weeks since he began the surveillance.

He got out of his car and walked down the street to the phone box and dialed her number, it rang for about three minutes without a reply.

Now he was really worried; putting the phone down he left the booth and ran back to the block of flats, as he climbed the steps he removed a card from his wallet. It read 'Gas Board;' he knocked on the janitors door and as the door opened he thrust the card under the man's nose.

'We've had a report of a leak in number twenty four,' he said, 'I've tried to gain entry, but there doesn't seem to be anyone there.'

'Hang on I'll get the keys,' said the man and went into his apartment to fetch them.

Together they went up the stairs and the man let him in; he sniffed and said to Reagan; 'doesn't seem to be any smell of gas.'

'No you're right, but I'd better make sure otherwise when they come back they'll put in a complaint; you know what they're like.'

The janitor nodded in commiseration; 'yeah; complain about the least little thing, tell me about it.'

The flat was empty, the bird had flown; but when and to where?

Coming down the stairs Reagan said, 'I don't suppose you would know when the occupants will return?'

'Oh there's only a young teacher living there; sort of keeps herself to her self if you know what I mean.'

He paused; 'wait a minute, I saw her leaving with a small suitcase earlier this evening, but then she normally does on a Monday, I think she goes to classes or something.'

Reagan thanked the man and hurried down the steps from the flats and returned to the phone booth.

He dialed a number and apprehensively started to explain.

Sheila Nicholson sped down the M4 towards London in her Mini Cooper; she had packed a few things and had left the apartment via the fire escape at the back of the block. There was a back way out of the car park into a parallel road and it had been easy to give the little 'Gum Shoe' the slip.' Cooper had rung her earlier that evening and apologized for being unable to send someone, but suggested the ruse she was now carrying out. She would book into a hotel for the night and then carry on to Norwich where he would meet her. He had been in her thoughts lately; a man who seemed more empathetic than most policemen she had met; he had a way with him that put her at her ease. She had not had many relationships with men and on the whole did not trust them; they usually only wanted one thing. She drove into the outskirts of London and found a Bed and Breakfast with parking for the car.

Next morning she traveled round the North Circular to Woodford then turned onto the A11 and headed for Norwich Strangely she felt quite elated; this unexpected adventure had roused her out of her normal routine and she was looking forward to whatever it had in store for her. As she passed through Loughton she was observed by a police car sitting in a side road; the driver spoke into his radio phone and then pulled out into the main road to shadow her. In a lay bye near the Saffron Walden turn off a large articulated lorry started up and joined the traffic flow towards Newmarket. The driver was in conversation with someone as he gained speed on the inside lane, 'a red Mini Cooper you say, what's the registration; right I'll keep a look out. 'He changed up through the gears and settled down at fifty miles an hour constantly glancing in his offside rear view mirror.

Sheila sped along the Motorway at a steady sixty in the outside lane; the traffic at this time of the morning was fairly light so she was making good time. She was looking forward to seeing Cooper again, he made her feel safe and secure somehow. Lights reflected in her rear view mirror she looked and saw a police car sitting on her tail, damn! The driver waved to her to move into the middle lane and let him past, she complied and as he tore past a lorry suddenly moved across in front of her into the middle lane and braked; instinctively she swerved to avoid him. She panicked and lost control; the Mini shot across the inside lane and over a steep embankment, rolling over and over as it plunged down the steep slope, finally coming to rest on it's roof on the torn up ground. The only sound was the ticking of the hot metal as the engine began to cool; there was no movement within the car.

CHAPTER NINETEEN

Cooper was worried; they had arranged to meet in Norwich Cathedral car park around eleven, it was now twelve thirty and there was still no sign of Sheila. What could have happened; he hoped it was maybe some problem like a puncture or a mechanical breakdown, but surely she would have phoned? He called Foley at the station and asked him to ring the AA and the RAC in case they had information of an accident.

As he paced up and down the Cathedral Close he heard his phone ringing and ran back to the car; it was Foley, 'there's been an accident on the A11 near Newmarket sergeant; I've got the registration number,' as he read it out Cooper's blood ran cold, it was Sheila's car.

'Is she all right?' there was a pause and Foley said, 'no I'm afraid not, they have taken her to Cambridge Hospital with serious injuries and that's all they have at the moment, I'm sorry Sarge.'

Cooper felt numb; he couldn't believe that they had caught up with her so soon, whatever resources had these people got?

Poor kid, she had been yet another victim of this awful series of events; even though she had no knowledge of what her father had been involved in. Obviously these people would stop at nothing to cover their tracks; he rang the Superintendent and put him in the picture.

He then drove to Cambridge and located the Hospital at Cherry Hinton; parking up he went to reception and showed his Warrant card. He was shown into a Waiting Room and a surgeon hurried in and introduced himself as Mr. Noonan.

'I'm afraid that she is still in a coma and will not be fit to be interviewed for the foreseeable future.'

'These things are not easy to gauge time wise; she has multiple injuries besides, in fact she is lucky to be alive.'

Cooper asked the surgeon if she would live.

'Well she's a fighter and if we can get the swelling down around the brain we have a good chance; her head is packed round with ice at the moment which should do the trick.' He shook Cooper's hand and said, 'give us a ring tomorrow and we will see how she's responding.'

Cooper left the hospital and phoned Foley again, 'could you ring Traffic and find out where the Mini was taken; also what happened to her personal things; handbag, suitcase and so on?'

He sat in the car and waited till Foley rang back; he might as well go and see what he could find while he was in the area.

Ten minutes later his phone rang and Foley gave him details of where the car was;

'Apparently the local boys haven't removed anything from the car yet,' he said

Cooper lit another cigarette and started the car; he headed for the Police station in Saffron Walden where the Mini had been taken. Arriving at the police station he showed his ID and explained why he wanted to see the wreck. After some interchange with the resident Inspector it was agreed that he could remove Sheila's personal effects providing they were returned after examination.

He was taken in a local Police car to the Pound; when he saw the wreck he was shocked; how she had survived the crash was nothing short of a miracle. The car was barely recognizable; just a tangled mass of twisted metal with the odd wheel sticking out here and there. They had to use cutting gear to open the boot and access the interior; eventually he had her bloodstained handbag and a badly crushed suitcase. He signed for them and thanked the local police for their help; carefully stowing the items in the boot of his car he set off on the return journey to Norwich.

Next morning after briefing the Superintendent he and Foley went through the contents of Sheila's handbag and suitcase.
It was an unpleasant job as the handbag was soaked in her blood; it contained all the usual women's things, make up, handkerchief, nail scissors etc. Her purse didn't yield anything of interest either, but Foley suddenly gave an exclamation as he withdrew an envelope from the suitcase.

'What have you got there Foley?' asked Cooper.

'Photos I think,' said the lad handing them over;
Cooper took the envelope in trembling fingers and removed the photographs and spread them out on the desk. He whistled to himself as he looked at them, they showed pictures of a group of Mercenaries with the stains of battle still on their fatigues.

'There; look Foley do you recognize him, it's Nicholson and there lurking in the background, that's Duffy.'

'These must have been taken after the action in Abundu; now we have a definite link between the two men.'
Cooper lit up another 'roll up' and smiled broadly, he leaned back in his chair putting his hands behind his head.

'You know what this means Foley, don't you, we shall soon be able to prove a connection between both men and Crown Oil.'

Foley looked doubtful; 'it's a pretty tenuous one Sergeant, they could say that the men were recruited by an independent organization on their behalf.'

He had a point; Cooper needed irrefutable proof that the hiring of the Mercenaries was done by someone within Crown Oil. Someone who knew both men and had probably arranged to get Duffy out of the mental institution in order for him to take part in the counter coup. Millington Smythe; it was all beginning to fall into place, he needed to obtain the man's military history somehow, but that wouldn't be easy. If he could establish previous contact by the three men during their service days it would prove they all knew each other.

He rang Sir Perry Warnes, his secretary answered; 'I'm sorry Detective Sergeant I'm afraid Sir Perry is on holiday in Scotland, can I take a message and get him to ring you when he returns?'

'Well you may be able to give me the information I need,' he said, 'whom do I ring to obtain details of a serviceman's Record of Service?'

There was a pause and then the secretary said, 'I'm sorry, but you would have to ask Sir Perry for that information, I don't have clearance at that level.'

Damn! There was that rigid official curtain descending again; 'when will Sir Perry be back?' he asked.

'I will ask him to contact you when he returns,' she answered primly and rang off.

Cooper fumed impotently, he felt that he was being given the run around by all and sundry at the moment and time was of the essence. Sheila must have found the photos and decided

76

to bring them with her to show him, poor girl she certainly didn't deserve to end up at death's door because of the machinations of a bunch of unscrupulous men. He rang the hospital and tried to talk to Noonan; but was told he was carrying out an operation; the Matron on Sheila's ward informed him that she was still in a coma, but was holding her own. Perhaps there was a way to find the information he needed; 'I shall be at the Reference Library Foley,' he said; putting on his coat and lighting up the inevitable cigarette he headed for the door

Cooper yawned and glanced at his watch, it was a quarter past four; he had been trawling through endless dailies from the fifties so far without success. It seemed that he would not be able to glean the information he wanted from this source. However he persevered and a few minutes later he struck gold; in the Daily Clarion he found an article about trouble in Yemen from tribal insurgents. It made particular reference to a special unit that had been sent out to deal with it and the C.O. was a certain Brigadier Millington Smythe. It also mentioned the Company that this unit was drawn from; better and better Cooper was delighted, he had found a possible link between the three men. All he had to do now to confirm that link was to contact the Army barracks of the Company with a view to obtaining further proof.

He went over to the information desk and requested a copy of the article to be made available to the police then went out into the street and gratefully lit up; six hours without a cigarette had been an ordeal. He had difficulty tracing their whereabouts; finally being informed that they had been merged with several other Regiments. However his informant mentioned that there was a Museum in Manchester that contained the Regalia, Standards and history of the Company. He contacted them and requested any photographic material relating to the action in Aden, with particular reference to the campaign in Yemen. They were reluctant to comply at first, but Cooper finally convinced the curator to co-operate promising that all the material would be returned. His jovial manner quite unnerved Foley who was more used to the usual calm demeanor his boss presented. Superintendent Trafford was impressed by Cooper's diligence; Munroe was not and tried to pour cold water on the new information.

'Ye canna take that as solid evidence; more like circumstantial stuff it seems to me, the man just happened to be in command of that particular group that's all.'

Cooper looked at him and said calmly, 'perhaps you have a better theory D.S. Munroe?'

'Ahm pursuing certain enquiries in a different direction at the moment and it has reached a critical stage; until I am in possession of all the facts I would rather not disclose what it is, said Munroe.

Trafford looked hard at the Scot and said, 'well perhaps if and when you decide to disclose it you will reveal it to us all, we shall be most grateful.'

His irony was lost on Munroe, who pulled himself up to his full height and remarked, 'Ye have no need to worry sir, when I have the full story you will be the first to hear it.'

The meeting came to a close and Trafford shook Cooper by the hand and said, 'keep up the good work,' turning to Munroe he remarked, 'I would appreciate a bit more urgency on your part Sergeant, this case has already made a large hole in the Force's budget.' Munroe smiled bleakly and strode purposefully out of the room; Cooper and Trafford exchanged meaningful glances though nothing was said.

CHAPTER TWENTY

Two days later Cooper received a phone call from Mr. Noonan the surgeon responsible for Sheila to inform him that she had regained consciousness.

'Can I talk to her?' asked Cooper.

'I don't see why not; as long as you don't tire her. 'Physically she is still weak, but she is rational and mentioned you by name.'

'I'll be over this afternoon if that's all right with you?' said Cooper.

.Sure that will be O.K.' said Noonan, 'I look forward to having a chat about her progress.'

He rang off and Cooper was left with a feeling of eager anticipation which had nothing to do with the interviewing of a victim of crime. He had a quick meal in the canteen and then set out for Cambridge arriving at the hospital around two.

Parking up he went through the glass doors to reception and showed his Warrant card; he was already expected, Noonan had left a message at the desk. He went up by lift to the second floor where the Recovery Wards were and entered Sheila's room. It was difficult to recognize her as she was swathed in bandages and both legs were in plaster. Her eyes were black and bloodshot and there was a scar which had left a white line through her left eyebrow.

She looked up as he entered and said; 'sorry I look such a mess; I hadn't expected to meet you looking like this.'

He laid down the large bunch of flowers on her bedside locker and pulled up a chair; 'I'm just grateful to see you alive,' he said, 'they obviously can work miracles in this place, when I came to see you last time it was touch and go.'

'You came to see me before?' she exclaimed, 'I suppose it was in an official capacity,' she smiled then winced as the bruising on her face hurt.

'No, as a matter of fact I felt personally responsible for you finishing up in here; if I had managed to get you protected this probably wouldn't have happened.'

They chatted inconsequentially for a while then he broached the subject of the crash.

'I can't remember much about it I'm afraid,' she said; 'except for this lorry pulling out in front of me and braking hard, after that it's a complete blank.'

'Well it's not important as we know most of the rest,' he said; then he went on to tell her about the photos found in her suitcase.

'Yes,' she replied; 'I came across them when I was packing; they had been in that drawer for ages and I thought that they might be of help in solving the case.'

'I can't thank you enough for them; they were the breakthrough we needed to connect your father and Duffy.

'They were the only photos that my father left me apart from the one in the frame; perhaps he had a reason for giving them to me,' she said thoughtfully.

'Well I'm glad he did,' observed Cooper; 'we would not have been able to make the progress we have without them.'

Just then Noonan bustled in holding out his hand he shook Cooper's and said, 'nice to see you again, glad to see you and our 'Wonder Girl' are getting on so well.'

'You will be pleased to know that she is progressing well and if she maintains the present rate of recovery we will be discharging her in a couple of week's time.'

'That's the best news I've heard this week;' smiled Cooper, he turned to Sheila and said, 'we shall have to organize somewhere for you to stay till the case is over as you are still at risk.' He drew Noonan to one side and explained the situation; the surgeon's eyes widened,

'You mean to say this was deliberate?'

Cooper nodded, 'that is why we have to take her into protective custody as they will try again.'

CHAPTER TWENTY ONE

Millington Smythe mopped his brow and reached for the bottle of tranquilizers in his desk drawer. Bowker had been raving at him again about the lack of closure of the Duffy debacle and the dumping of Crown Oil shares on the market by some of their largest shareholders. The Press was beginning to smell blood and was asking searching questions about the stability of the company despite the reassurances he had issued.

'If you can't stop the rot we will have to find someone who can;' Bowker had shouted down the phone, slamming it down without giving him the chance to reply.

He was not sleeping well and his wife had joined his critics saying that he had to get a grip or if he lost his position she would have to consider hers! He took out a small black book and thumbed through the pages; finding what he was looking for he picked up the phone and dialed a number in Southern Ireland.

'Hello Shaun, I have a job for you here in England we need to meet;' he continued the conversation making the necessary arrangements for a rendezvous.

Shaun Murphy was someone that Millington Smythe had used during his spell in Northern Ireland; sometimes for procuring information and for the occasional execution when the target was too prominent in the community for direct action by other methods. He had contacts on both sides and moved easily around the Bogside without suspicion; he had been a valuable asset to the Authorities and the Security Services alike. Murphy had bought a farm in County Mayo with his blood money and settled down to the rural life.

The call had come out of the blue and he put the phone down, lit a cigarette and reflected whether he should put himself in the frame for this hit. The money was good; but the risk of killing a policeman in England gave him pause for thought.

He considered long and hard, but in the end greed prevailed and he began to plan his course of action Firstly he could not risk smuggling weaponry into the UK, so he would have to arrange for his requirements to be waiting for him when he arrived.

His old dog whimpered in its sleep as it lay by the hearth its legs twitching as if it were chasing a rabbit. He bent down and stroked its ears and it slipped into a deeper sleep; he was fond of the animal and considered dogs much more dependable than people.

His wife came through from the kitchen wiping her hands on a tea cloth; 'who was that calling Shaun, was it mother?'

'No darlin' twas just a feller I used to know back in the old days he just rang me for the crack.'

She frowned; 'I hope it's not someone wantin' you to do something illegal; you promised me all that was behind you when we moved here.'

He laughed, 'Mary you have an over active imagination; some feller rings me up and you immediately tink' I'm goin' to bump somebody off..'

'As a matter of fact he's invited me over to England for the fishin' all paid for; so I couldn't nicely say no now could I?'

She nodded, but her eyes were still wary; 'no I suppose you couldn't; how long will you be?'

'Ah, just a few days unless the fishin' is really good; I'll ring ye darlin' every night and tell ye how things are goin.'

With that he kissed her on the cheek and put on his waterproof jacket and cap; whistling the dog he walked to the front door and went out into the rain.

CHAPTER TWENTY TWO

Two weeks later Cooper drew up outside the hospital in an unmarked police car, he glanced around the car park as he got out and then went into the Reception area.

Showing his ID card he was directed to an annex down an adjacent corridor where Sheila was waiting with two brand new traveling cases.

'Are you ready?' said Cooper as he picked up the cases; she nodded eagerly and they went out to the car.

He stowed the cases in the boot; made sure she was comfortable then jumped in the car, they swept out of the car park and he was soon heading for the Baldock Road.

'This place you are going to is a bit remote,' he said; 'but we will take you out now and then so you don't get too bored.'

'Will you be coming to do that?' she said looking at him.

'Sometimes; when I can get away,' he replied, 'but as you can imagine things are a bit hectic at the moment.'

'We have someone who will be on call twenty four hours every day whilst you are there so you have no need to feel lonely.'

'Who's that?' she asked.

'W.P.C. Gaskell, she's about your age and has a jolly personality, so she can cheer you up when things get a bit fraught.'

'How long do you think this situation will go on for?' she asked.

'Once we get the answers to certain questions we can close the case and you will be able to pick up your life again,' he replied.

She looked him in the face for several moments as if she was trying to discover the answers there, then she shrugged resignedly and lit up a cigarette. Cooper drove through Baldock on the A10 and after about fifteen minutes turned off down a leafy country lane. Eventually the road wound up a steep hill and on reaching the top he turned into a long drive lined with mature beech trees. As the car reached the end it swept into a large flagstone forecourt fronting a magnificent Georgian house.

Sheila was impressed, 'is this place I'm going to stay at?' she said incredulously.

Cooper grinned, 'I hate to disappoint you; but you will be staying over there,' he pointed to a series of garages.

'There's a very nice apartment over the top,' he said; you should have ample room and we can guarantee top security there, the house is just too large.'

He took her bags out of the boot and said, 'come on and I'll introduce you to Molly;' she followed him to the stairs leading up to the apartment.

Standing at the top smiling was her bodyguard and companion W.P.C. Gaskell; Sheila noticed that the woman was wearing a side arm that brought home to her the seriousness of her situation. Cooper called out a greeting to Molly and introduced her to Sheila. He took the suitcases in.

87

CHAPTER TWENTY THREE

Shaun Murphy took the ferry over to Hollyhead and kept his head down as he went through reception to avoid the cameras. He arrived in London in the late afternoon after having traveled down by train; jumping into a taxi he told the driver to drop him off at the Hilton The cabby looked at him and turning away raising his eyebrows as he pulled out of the station and headed for the West End; his fare didn't look like someone who would stay at the Hilton. He was traveling on one of several passports under the name of O'Shaunessy, posing as a salesman for one of the small publishers in Dublin. Once at the hotel he changed; bathed and shaved and sat down to await his instructions from Millington Smythe.

The call came through about six pm, 'the Chairman sounded stressed; 'things not going according to plan,' asked Murphy?

There was a slight pause at the other end of the line and then Millington Smythe answered; 'Oh, no nothing to worry about Shaun,' Murphy noticed the forced joviality and drew his own conclusions.

He then outlined the details of the hit and told Murphy to pick up the contents of a locker at Kings Cross station.

Murphy said, 'I trust my fee will be there too; for the books?'

'Of course and on a satisfactory conclusion there will be a bonus payable.'

At the end of the conversation Murphy lay on the bed smoking and looking at the ceiling, he was beginning to feel that all was not as it should be in this business and things were going on that he should know about. He got off the bed, stubbed out his cigarette and picked up the phone; he rang one of his journalist friends whom he had met in Ireland during the troubles.

'Hallo Dennis, Shaun here; I'm over here doing a little job for your Security people; I wondered if you could meet me for dinner, it's on me.'

He knew that Dennis would scent a story and be only to keen to accept and so it proved. Two hours later he met Dennis Quilly in the foyer and they went through to the dining room.

During the meal they talked about old times in Northern Ireland until Murphy worked round to the subject of Crown Oil.

'I have a few shares in the Company, but I'm a bit worried as they seem not to be doin' so well Dennis, do you think I should sell?'

Dennis stopped with his fork in mid air; slowly he looked at Murphy and said, 'you're the second person who has asked me that this week, one hears rumours about changes in the boardroom, but I will have to ask our Business correspondent he has his ear to the ground in these matters.' He tried to pump Murphy about his mission in England; but the Irishman held up his hand and said; 'you know the form on these things Dennis, but I will give you somethin' when it's finished.' They parted

amicably with Quilly promising to let Shaun know what
he could glean from his colleague regarding the
Murphy went down to the underground car park and
unlocked the hire car that he had ordered; it was a dark blue
Ford Escort, he got in and drove out into the street.

CHAPTER TWENTY FOUR

Sheila Nicholson walked through the grounds with a security dog handler fifty yards behind her; this had become her routine since being brought to this place of safety. She wished Cooper would come and see her he had not been in touch for two weeks and despite the efforts of her Police companion Molly she was becoming stir crazy. He had said that she would be taken out from time to time, but so far it hadn't happened. Mind you the grounds of this place were magnificent with terracing that went right down to the river and the views across the countryside were breathtaking, but most of the time the nagging fear of someone making an attempt on her life kept surfacing from her subconscious. When would he return; she felt safe with him, he made the fear go away somehow; she smiled wistfully, Sheila you're falling for him, be careful, she thought to herself as she climbed the stairs to her place of incarceration. Molly was vacuuming the place as she let herself in; Sheila couldn't help smiling it was so incongruous seeing an armed police woman carrying out such a mundane chore. She went into the kitchen and made two coffees, then carried them through signaling to Molly to join her.

'How are you this morning?' Molly inquired.

'In need of a break; this is beginning to get to me,' replied Sheila, 'when will DS. Cooper be back, he said something about me getting out sometime.'

Molly chuckled, 'I think you have a soft spot for Dan; trouble is he is so wrapped up with his work since his wife left him that he barely notices anything outside of police matters. 'I'll give him a ring if you like and see if he can tear himself away to take you shopping in Cambridge or somewhere, how about that?'

Sheila visibly brightened; 'that would be lovely, thanks Molly you're a friend in need.' 'When did his wife leave him,' she asked?

'Oh, about three years ago; like so many policemen's wives the loneliness got the better of her so she found someone else; it's a familiar story I'm afraid.'

Sheila thought she heard a note of regret in Molly's voice, 'are you married Molly?'

'I was; trouble is Dan's situation doesn't just apply to men; my hubby decided he needed a younger model, one that wasn't out on duty all hours of the day or night.'

'So you see members of the police force are not a sensible option if you want a stable and settled relationship.'

Molly was as good as her word and Cooper managed to come and pick her up a few days later and took her over to Cambridge. They walked through the centre of the old town and he took her to lunch in a lovely old world pub overlooking the river. It was a sunny day and the sight of the swans waiting for diners to throw them some bread or the occasional passing punt with young students enjoying the idyll of youth and each others company filled her with envy. She looked at Cooper, he looked tired; she felt a moment of guilt, in her selfish desire for his company she had not thought of the strain he must be under trying to bring this case to a conclusion.

'Have I been too demanding?' she asked; he looked surprised by the question.

'What do you mean,' he said, 'here we are sitting by the banks of the Cam on a beautiful day giving me a chance to forget about work and having the pleasure of your company, that's no hardship.'

Murphy kept his distance from the couple as they strolled through the streets of Cambridge; he had waited outside the Norwich police headquarters till Cooper had emerged and got into his car,. After that it had been a simple matter of following at a safe distance till they arrived at the 'safe house.' When Cooper drove out of the gate with the woman aboard he tagged along to see where they were going; during their lunch he walked a little way down the bank of the Cam where he could keep an eye on them. He had bought himself some sandwiches and ate them whilst waiting for the couple to move off; occasionally throwing pieces of bread to the swans. He was not intending to attempt a hit in this crowded place as he preferred to use a rifle with a scope for such matters. They seemed very happy together thought Murphy, such a pity that he had to spoil things; but then one had to earn a crust in this wicked world.

They left Cambridge on the return journey around four; Sheila clutching her bag of shopping and feeling happy. As they drove along the A10 Cooper glanced in his rear view mirror; there was that dark blue Escort again; it was keeping several cars between them, but was obviously following.

He said nothing to Sheila; he didn't want to alarm her unnecessarily, also he didn't want to alert his 'tail' that he

93

knew he was being followed. Who could it be; as far as he knew only him and the 'Super' knew where the safe house was, he had insisted on this on a need to know basis. He would get Sheila back to safety and then deal with whoever it was that was shadowing them. They arrived back and Cooper got her inside the flat; drawing Molly on one side he told her of the situation.

'Do you think it could be someone planning to kill Sheila?' asked Molly.

'We must work on that assumption,' said Cooper; 'will you alert all the staff here to be on their guard and I'll try and get to the bottom of this?'

'Also I think it would be wise to keep things to ourselves for the time being; what worries me is how this guy knew where she was; is he being briefed by someone inside the Force?'

He drove thoughtfully up the drive, stopping fifty yards before the gate he slipped into the undergrowth beside the driveway and moved slowly towards the perimeter wall.

Pulling himself up to the top he dropped over onto the outside and looked up and down the road. Sure enough there was the Escort parked on the verge just out of sight of anyone emerging from the gate. He walked towards it noting the registration, as he neared the car he could see the car was empty. He turned the car around and headed back to the House; jumping out of the car he ran up the stairs to the flat and hammered on the door. Molly looked through the small window before letting him in; she had drawn her pistol and was ready for action.

'Where's Sheila?' he shouted.

'In the loft space," replied Molly, 'do you want me to get her to come down?'

'No leave her there till we find this damned intruder,' he was angry with himself for not foreseeing this development; they were on the back foot with a potential assassin somewhere on the Estate.

He went over to the Hall where the rest of the guards were based; there was only a P.C. there manning the phone, the rest of the group were out hunting the intruder. As he came out he heard a shot from the shrubbery at the back of the house and ran round. One of the dog handlers was standing over his German shepherd; the dog had been shot and was dying.

Cooper shouted; 'where is he?'

The man pointed in the direction of the woods adjacent to the Hall, 'they followed him in there,' Cooper noticed that the man was crying.

He ran into the wood and could hear the sounds of a pursuit ahead of him, there were two more shots followed by silence.

He reached a clearing where an officer sat nursing a bleeding leg; 'which way did he go?' shouted Cooper, 'through there,' indicated the man pointing.

'Hang on; I'll get someone to you as soon as I can,' shouted Cooper as he turned and ran along a narrow path that led through the wood.

There was a body lying across the path, it was another officer; Cooper stopped and turned the body over, the man had been shot through the head. The man still had his pistol in his hand, Cooper gently removed it, checked that it was loaded and turned and continued to run along the path. He arrived at the wall quite near to where he had gone over earlier; stuffing the pistol into his coat pocket he shinned over the wall and dropped to the ground just in time to see the Escort gunning up the road. By the time he had extricated the pistol from his pocket the car was out of range and he was left fuming with rage; it had been a fiasco and he was responsible. He walked back to the injured man; fortunately the bullet had gone through the fleshy part of his calf and Cooper bound the wound as best he could and supported the limping officer back to the Hall. He called in and reported to Trafford then rang for a local ambulance to take the injured man to hospital and a police van to remove the dead officer. He managed to get a description of the intruder from the officer before the ambulance arrived.

'He was a wiry looking fellow with dark hair and a long face, he was using a small automatic, I think it was a Beretta, and he certainly knew how to use it.'

'Where's Chris, he asked,' is he all right, I heard another shot after I was hit?'

Cooper looked away, 'I'm afraid he wasn't so lucky,' he said and went on to explain what had happened.

The man was devastated; 'he and I have worked together ever since leaving Hendon,' he said,

'Who's going to tell his missus; they've got two lovely kids as well, Oh my God.'

He put his hand over his face and shook his head, 'I never thought to see this happen to Chris; I know the job can be dangerous, but when it's close to home..,' he subsided into silence.

Cooper put a hand on his shoulders; 'rest assured he won't get away with it. I promise that we will hunt him down with the whole force of the Law.'

Later he went back to see how Sheila and Molly had coped with things; Sheila was subdued at first, but gradually perked up as Cooper talked to her.

'We shall have to consider moving you again Sheila; this place is no longer secure and we don't want a repeat performance of today's events.' 'I have already discussed a move with my superior officer and he agrees it should be done as soon as possible; so I shall be stopping over tonight with a view to moving you tomorrow, I don't expect our friend to return to have another go in the near future.'

She looked at her hands and said, 'it seems to me that the price of keeping me safe is too high; that poor man that was killed had a family, what will happen to them?'

'They will be well provided for by the Police Welfare system as far as income is concerned,' replied Cooper; 'it won't make up for his loss of course, but every officer knows the risks of the job'.

'It won't make up for the loneliness of his widow or how his children will miss him either,' she said.

He couldn't think of a suitable response, so he bade them goodnight and retired to bed; it had been an eventful day.

CHAPTER TWENTYFIVE

Early next morning she had her bags packed and by seven thirty they were on their way to the next hideaway. It was a beautiful morning and as the car sped through the countryside Sheila felt her spirits rise; just to be free and driving to who knew where with Dan was enough to cheer her.

'We should be there in a couple of hours;' he said, 'it's not such a grand venue, but it is easier to defend should it be necessary.'

'Will they try again?' she asked.

'Hard to say,' said Cooper; 'the guy has made one attempt and left a policeman dead and another wounded, he must know that we will move Heaven and Earth in order to catch him.' 'It depends on how desperate he is to earn his money; which must be considerable to risk killing policemen.'

She shuddered involuntarily; the thought of someone deliberately trying to kill her sent a chill down her back.

Cooper turned and looked at her; he grinned engagingly and said,

'Try not to worry; look at that wonderful world out there, it wasn't made for worrying.'

She managed a smile, but it wasn't reflected in her eyes.

The next time Cooper looked her way he saw she was asleep; 'probably reaction to the stress,' he murmured, 'best thing in the circumstances.'

He passed through Attleborough and headed down the A11 towards Norwich; reaching the outskirts he cut through to get on to the coastal road to Yarmouth. Through Acle he turned off onto a minor road and began crossing the marshes where cattle from all over the United Kingdom were sent to be fattened up on the nourishing pastures of the region.

Sheila awoke and rubbed her eyes, looking round she said, 'where on earth are we?'

It certainly appeared to be an alien landscape; flat marsh land stretched out in all directions interspersed with a network of dykes which kept the grassland moist.

There were also the sails of yachts dotted along the river Yare which was bounded on both sides by high banks to prevent flooding in the winter months. He pointed to a house looking small and remote across the fields,

'There is where we are heading, it's called appropriately 'Marsh man's Cottage.'

'It looks like something out of a horror film;' she said pulling a face, 'one could almost see Boris Karloff lurching across the fields in search of some unfortunate victim.'

He laughed; 'you have an over active imagination young lady, you'll feel better after a cup of tea.'

He pulled up beside a five barred gate and producing a key unlocked it, opened the gate and drove through, stopping to shut and lock the gate again. He followed a muddy track which had been shaped by generations of tractor wheels into an undulating quagmire. The car rolled and lurched across it

like a ship on a bad day in the Bay of Biscay, Sheila began to feel quite queasy as the motion continued.
A large herd of Friesians chewed contentedly as they watched the car's progress across the field.

'Do we have to endure this every time we come and go?' she gasped, holding on to the dashboard.

'You'll get used to it,' he said; 'it's called living in the country, some people quite like it!'

'They must be deranged;' she muttered, 'call this living; survival would be nearer the mark.'

Just then they hit a collection of bricks that had been put down by the farmer in a particularly muddy spot. Sheila took off and bumped her head on the roof and landed back again in her seat uttering words that would have mystified her small pupils.

Cooper gave a hoot of laughter and slowed down; 'are you all right?' he inquired mischievously?

Her reply was unintelligible; eventually they reached the old cottage which was situated next to the river. She crawled painfully out of the car and checked herself out for injuries; much to her annoyance she seemed to be unscathed apart from bruising on her nether regions. Cooper unlocked the front door which swung open with a creaking groan; he made an exaggerated bow and said,

'Welcome to your home from home modom.'

She stuck out her tongue and with her head held high she walked through the door and collided with the umbrella stand.

The place smelt musty and there were cobwebs in the hall; 'when was the last time this place was lived in,' she said as she picked up sticks and umbrellas and returned them to the stand.

'Ten years ago; the lady who owned it was a commercial pilot and we acquired it for the purpose it is now being used for,' he explained.

He went into the kitchen and switched on the electricity which proceeded to give out a menacing humming sound. He searched through the wall cupboards until he found some cups; he filled the kettle and stuck it on the hob, then he rinsed the cups and found a packet of tea..

'I've only got a tin of Carnation milk, will that do?' he called out.

'I suppose so;' she replied resignedly, surely things couldn't get any worse?

He brought the tea through and they sat down in the lounge to drink it; she looked around the room it had a sort of rustic charm, but needed a lot of work to bring it up to her standards.

'What do you think?' said Cooper, "or shouldn't I ask.'

'I think that I will have to spend the foreseeable future trying to make it habitable,' she remarked.

'Oh come on it's not that bad, just needs a woman's touch; he said, 'the basics are all there.'

'Basic is exactly right, the whole place is basic that's the trouble; no wonder the last occupant left.'

He shrugged and walked over to the window just in time to see a Land Rover bumping along the track towards the cottage.

'Here comes the Cavalry,' he quipped, 'just in the nick of time I think.'

The vehicle pulled up outside the front door and three people got out; Molly was the first to enter followed by a large policeman and finally a dog handler with a German shepherd dog straining at the leash.

Molly hugged Sheila and they began an animated conversation; Cooper greeted the other two, 'Hallo Ben,' he said shaking the large officer by the hand, 'nice to see you again,' he turned to the dog handler, 'and you are?'

'PC Wendling,' he responded, 'and this is Bullet,' he said waving a hand at the dog; he pricked up his ears on hearing his name.

Sheila noticed that all three were wearing side arms and Ben was carrying a pump action shotgun. They had obviously arrived prepared for trouble; she could feel her anxiety level beginning to rise.

'This place is certainly remote;' said Ben, 'but it should be easy to defend there's no cover anywhere near the house; I suppose the only real threat could be from the river.'

Cooper glanced at Sheila; he could see that Ben's line of conversation was making her more nervous.

'Shall we have a look round the place?' he said steering Ben outside, the dog handler followed them.

'Go easy with the 'shop talk' the girl is frightened enough already without us adding to it.'

'Ben looked embarrassed; 'sorry boss I didn't think.'

'O.K. Ben, but try not to make her any more jumpy than she is at present.'

He walked around to the back of the house where the river bank stood about four feet from the ground. There were steps cut into it to enable access to the river, he climbed up and saw there was a rowing boat moored to a wooden platform let into the side of the bank. This meant that they had means of escape to the other side of the river if the need arose.

102

There was a small shed at the side of the cottage and PC Wendling decided it would be suitable for Bullet's accommodation. Finally the officers unloaded the supplies and additional arms and ammunition from the Land Rover and settled in.

CHAPTER TWENTY SIX

After a meal Cooper said his farewells and drove back to Norwich much to Sheila's dismay; she knew that he had to continue his investigations, but resented that his duties took him away from her.

Foley had news for him when he arrived, 'they've found that Ford Escort, it had been abandoned in a back street in Pimlico.'

'Anything in the car that could help us?' said Cooper.

'Forensics is still working on it, but nothing so far; it had been wiped clean by whoever was driving. 'One thing though, the registration; it's a hire car, apparently the guy who rented it was Irish.'

'What name was it registered in?' said Cooper pricking up his ears.

'O'Shaunessy; but I bet that wasn't his real name,' said Foley.

Cooper sighed; 'It would be nice to be on a straightforward robbery with violence or a domestic, this case has so many twists and turns it makes me dizzy.'

He picked up the phone and rang a friend in Customs at Hollyhead.

'Hallo Phillip I'm on a case at the moment which involves an Irishman, have you had anyone interesting through in the last few days?'

Phillip thought for a few moments; 'what has this guy been up to Dan?'

'He has killed one policeman and wounded another in an attempt to hit a potential witness.'

The Customs officer gave a low whistle, 'we haven't had anything like that for a while; look give me a bit of time to check and I'll get back to you, OK?'

Cooper put down the phone and started to catch up with his mail; his in tray was piled high. A large manila envelope caught his eye; he opened it and was thrilled to see the contents, they were the photos he had been promised from the Regimental museum in Manchester.' He began to look through them; but in the main they were of groups of soldiers from the Regiment that the section led by Millington Smythe had been seconded to. He was down to the last two when suddenly there they were. It was slightly out of focus, but he could see Nicholson sitting in the front row with Millington Smythe in the centre and Duffy in the second row; Bingo.

Foley couldn't believe his eyes as his boss leapt to his feet and began to dance around the room.

'I've got it Foley; this photo proves the link between Millington Smythe and the other two.'

CHAPTER TWENTY SEVEN

Murphy sat in the café across the street from the Norwich police headquarters; since the foiled attempt on Cooper's life he had changed his appearance, now he sported a blonde wig, dark glasses and a moustache. He sipped his third coffee slowly and re-capped the events of the past few days; it had been a close run thing getting away from the safe house, t'was a pity that he had to shoot the two policemen, but as Napoleon had once said, 'you can't make an omelet without breaking eggs.' He was well aware of the risks he was taking being this close to the police; but unless and until he could find out where the girl had been taken he couldn't complete his contract. Perhaps he should just dispose of Cooper and ignore the girl; but Millington Smythe had stipulated both parties in his briefing and Murphy preferred a satisfied client. Just as he drank up and prepared to leave who should come down the steps of the headquarters but Cooper.

Murphy paid up and hurried round the corner to his replacement car; a beige Morris Oxford, getting in he watched till Cooper drove out of the car park and he eased out behind, they weaved through the morning traffic till Cooper joined the Yarmouth road. As they drove down the road Murphy opened the glove compartment and checked that the Ouzi machine gun was in place. It was part of the equipment that had been provided for him and was small and reliable, a favorite choice of the Israeli army. He kept well back as they headed for the new Safe House; Cooper turned off the Yarmouth road and Murphy carried on for about a mile then backed into a gateway and turned round, taking the turning that Cooper had gone down. He didn't want to get too close; as he came round a bend he spotted Cooper's car bumping across the marsh track and drove past until he reached the river. He parked up the car and slung a pair of powerful binoculars around his neck; there was a track running along the top of the river bank going in the direction of where Cooper had left the road, Murphy started along it. He saw Marshman's Cottage standing like a lone sentinel down the track, also he noted that there was a Land Rover outside as well as Cooper's car. Slipping off the bank on the landward side he stole forward till he came to a gateway that led into a field adjacent to the cottage which provided him with cover whilst he surveyed the place .Training the glasses on the front of the cottage he could see movement through the windows; as far as he could make out there were at least three people inside. He stiffened as he saw a dog handler complete with a large male German shepherd come round the side of the cottage. Fortunately the wind was blowing towards him so the dog didn't pick up his scent and they carried on across the marsh. The dog would have to be eliminated from the equation when he returned otherwise he would lose the element of surprise. He considered that he had seen enough for the time being and slipped away back to the car; he had to prepare for the attack and there were several things he needed to acquire.

CHAPTER TWENTY EIGHT

Cooper was not happy with the security aspect of the cottage; he still thought that it was vulnerable from the river.

He drew Ben to one side and confided his thoughts on the matter; 'someone could land behind the cottage from a small craft and be on us before we had time to react,' he mused, 'we need someone guarding that area, particularly at night.'

'Surely Bullet would suss' them and give us warning?' said Ben, 'that's what he's here for after all.'

'That's true,' admitted Cooper; 'but dogs can be dealt with one way and another.'

'Alec and I will patrol in shifts with the dog,' said Ben, 'that should cover it; so that will leave two of us in the house at all times.'

Cooper nodded in agreement, 'yeah that seems satisfactory; OK Ben I'll love you and leave you I must get back to the office there are things I have to do.'

He said his goodbyes and drove back to the gate; as he was unlocking it a beige Morris Oxford flashed past and he caught a glimpse of the driver, he was wearing dark glasses; Cooper thought that odd as the day was overcast' He was unable to catch the registration of the vehicle as it was being driven at high speed he shrugged and put it from his mind.

There was a message from Phillip Cronshaw to ring him back which he immediately did; 'I think I may have something for you Dan re-your Irishman,' the Customs official said. 'I had a look through the photographs taken last week by the security cameras and I spotted someone who is well known to us; he kept his head down as he came through, but unfortunately the officer on duty is new otherwise we would have stopped him.'

'Who is it?' said Cooper impatiently.

'A certain Shaun Murphy, he must be traveling on a false passport.'

'What's his background?' inquired Cooper.

'Freelance assassin and fixer; he made money from both sides during the 'Troubles' and retired to a farm in Mayo.'

Cooper's heart sank, this guy seemed even worse that Nicholson or Duffy, he must warn his team at the cottage it seemed that an attack was imminent.

'I took the liberty of contacting the Guarda in Mayo to see if he was at home, they made discreet enquiries and apparently he is supposed to be on a fishing holiday in England,' said Phillip.

'Phil' you've been a great help I owe you,' said Cooper: he put down the phone and shouted to Foley, 'I've got to get back to the cottage; tell the Superintendent that we have another hit attempt coming up and I have got to warn them.'

Apart from being remote the place had no phone so it was imperative that he returned to oversee the situation. As he drove out to the cottage the image of that beige car flashed into his mind; could that have been Murphy and had he been casing the place?

CHAPTER TWENTY NINE

Murphy glanced at the clock in his hotel room; it was coming up to eight pm, he was wearing dark clothing and stuffed a balaclava and black leather gloves into a pocket. He had been busy after returning from his surveying of the safe house; visiting several sports shops he eventually found what he was looking for in an Army and Navy store. He went down to the underground car park and unlocked the boot of his car; there was a military back pack containing the Ouzi, his Beretta automatic and a lightweight rifle assembly complete with night scope. He was carrying a commando stiletto in case silence was needed; there was also a mysterious large carrying case stowed in the boot. Murphy checked everything and grunted with satisfaction; closing the boot lid he got into the car and drove up the ramp and out into the night.

Arriving at the river he pulled off the road into a grassy lane; opening the boot he heaved out the large case and dragged it down to the river bank. Opening the case he revealed a one man folding kayak which he quickly assembled, fitting the twin paddles together. He then went back to the car and took out the back pack; he looked at the luminous dial of his watch, ten thirty, he was a bit early.

No matter, he could still paddle up the river and wait; he lowered the craft into the water tied the back pack behind the seat and climbed aboard. There was no moon; the sky was still overcast as he paddled upstream towards his goal, good that's one thing in my favor, he thought. The water lapped at the sides of the kayak as he cut through the water; the tranquility being occasionally broken by the lowing of cattle or the sound of some nocturnal bird.

He pulled into the bank about fifty yards away from the cottage and sat and listened; he could smell cigarette smoke coming from the direction of the bank behind it, there was obviously a guard there. Where was the dog? That was the million dollar question, presumably with the guard; he took a small parcel from the pack and slipped it inside his jacket.
The wind was blowing towards him hence his being able to smell the cigarette smoke; he eased himself out of the kayak onto the bank ensuring it was securely moored. Slipping over the bank he cautiously approached the cottage stopping now and then to listen; the smell of smoke was stronger now so he knew he was not far from the officer on guard. He lowered himself carefully onto the ground and looked up at the bank; silhouetted against the sky he could see the man looking out across the river.

Alec Wendling flicked the stub of his cigarette and watched it arc into the river with a brief hiss as it met the water; he never knew who had killed him as Murphy drove the stiletto down through his left shoulder into his heart. Grabbing the man's shoulders he lowered him into the river and watched his pale face recede as he sank slowly into the depths.
Murphy heard a low growl behind him and turned slowly; the dog had found him!

111

CHAPTER THIRTY

As Cooper drew up outside the cottage Ben came out to greet him; 'hello boss we didn't think we'd be seeing you so soon,' seeing his face Ben asked, 'what's up?'

'Full alert Ben we will be having a visitor; most probably tonight.'

'Ben looked grim, "right boss I'll call Alec and Molly I expect you'll want a word.'

They discussed what they would need to do and the men began to patrol the grounds with Bullet.

Cooper went round the house checking the doors and windows; these were old but sturdy and fitted with iron fixtures. Whoever tried to break into the house would have to make a lot of noise getting in.

He shouted down the stairs, 'Sheila can you make us a cup of tea, I'm parched and I expect Molly could do with one.'

She went into the kitchen and put the kettle on; she felt more secure now he was here, he inspired confidence.

The sun was beginning to set behind the trees throwing the branches in to sharp relief and a large bank of cloud advanced heralding the end of day and advancing night. Cooper drew all the curtains and switched on the lights; he was now carrying a police automatic which Ben had provided.

His guess was that Murphy would wait until after midnight before making his move to try and gain maximum surprise.

Well they could do nothing more except await developments; he wished he had a few more men at his disposal, but he had great respect for those he had. Sheila provided them with pizzas and they gratefully consumed them, at least they would not go into the fray hungry.

Alec stood up and reached for his jacket; 'I'll go and feed Bullet and then take the first shift at the river bank,' turning to Ben he said, 'don't forget to relieve me at twelve Ben.'

He went out in to the gathering gloom and Cooper locked the door behind him, turning to Ben he said, 'I'll take the second shift so you can get your head down.'

'Thanks boss, much appreciated; I think I'll go up now if you don't mind,' Cooper shook his head and Ben made for the stairs.

The three remaining chatted in a desultory manner, each knowing that their lives would probably never be the same again; Cooper suggested a game of cards and managed to find a well worn pack in the sideboard drawer. They took turns in playing Whist, Gin Rummy and even Four Card Stud, but their heart was not in it. Finally the old Grandfather clock in the hall struck midnight and Cooper threw down his cards and stood up.

'Duty calls folks,' he remarked; 'I had better go and wake Alec up.'

Molly laughed; 'that's not fair Dan, he is one of the most conscientious officers I know.'

'He'll probably be grateful for cups of coffee when he arrives,' said Cooper, 'cheerio, see you later.'

CHAPTER THIRTY ONE

Murphy stood stock still while the dog looked at him still growling softly; it was a mercy that it had not barked. He started to talk quietly to it whilst slowly reaching for the parcel in his inside pocket; taking it out he removed the paper revealing a piece of prime steak. He tossed it to Bullet who ignored it at first; but the wonderful odour of the meat was tempting and finally the dog gulped it down. The growl gradually subsided and then the dog sat down suddenly, shook his head then rolled on his side uttering a low whine and lay motionless. Murphy realized that he was soaked in sweat; he mopped his brow, God he had been lucky; this feller could have torn his throat out. The dog would be out for several hours and would wake up with nothing more than a hangover; he didn't like killing animals, but the previous time the dog had got too close for comfort. He went back to the kayak and untied his pack; slipping it on he returned to the cottage and carefully moved around the outside examining it. He had just got to the shed when he heard the cottage door open; the door of the shed was ajar and he quickly slipped inside. Cooper came round the corner and walked towards the back of the house; damn, thought Murphy he must be goin' to relieve the other guy. He slipped out of the shed and into the trees beside the house to rethink his plan of campaign.

He had to know where everyone was and now it had all gone wrong; Cooper was bound to see the dog, put two and two together and raise the alarm. He had to do something to get them all together, preferably out of the house. He made a dash around to the front of the house and took two items out of his pack; they were military incendiaries he put one through the letter box and threw the second one through a bedroom window then as the bombs exploded and began to burn he hurried into the darkness. Cooper had just discovered the dog when he heard the explosions; he dashed back the way he had come when there was a burst of automatic fire and he dived for cover.

He crawled back the way he had come then stood up and sprinted round to the back of the house.
Picking up the dustbin he hurled it through the kitchen window and climbed in; shouting, 'don't shoot it's me,' he ran into the hallway.
The fire had already taken hold and flames were roaring up the walls; ignoring the heat he ran into the lounge; Molly and Sheila were cowering at the back of the room.
'Come on we have to get out of the back; he's waiting for us to run out of the front so he can gun us down.'
He pulled down one of the drapes and said, 'cover yourselves with this and run like hell; I've got to get Ben.'
'Make for the boat and get across the river it's the only chance;' he heard glass shattering upstairs God surely the fire isn't up there already;" he ran up the stairs and opened the main bedroom door,.
A gout of flame reached out for him and he staggered back; 'are you there Ben?' he shouted; no reply.

The heat was becoming unbearable as he went to the next bedroom; there was Ben lying on the bed he had been overcome by fumes.

He grabbed him, pulled him off the bed and dragged him to the rear of the cottage; fortunately the fire had not spread to that area yet. Cooper opened the window and looked out; there was an extension roof over the kitchen and he managed to get Ben onto the window sill and lower him onto the tiles of the sloping roof below. He followed him out and lowered him to the ground; by now the place was well alight and windows were cracking and exploding with the heat.

How he managed to get Ben into the dingy he would never know; the two women were already in so he cast off and started rowing for the other side. The flames were reflecting off the water as he pulled for the opposite shore; suddenly there was a burst of machine gun fire and bullets were spraying overhead. The bastard had guessed that they had got out and was hell bent on finishing his diabolical work.
'Get down, get down, it's your only chance;' he shouted rowing as fast as he could for the opposite bank. Suddenly the firing stopped, what the..., then he realized either Murphy's gun had jammed or he had emptied the clip .He redoubled his efforts and they reached the bank; 'jump and run for your lives,' he shouted as he made the boat fast and then pulled Ben out of the boat. The firing recommenced, but it was not on target because of the darkness and he managed to drag his colleague away from the river. Ben started to come round and after a coughing fit he managed to stand up;
'What the hell happened' he said?

'It's a long story,' said Cooper; 'come on let's find a phone and get some help.' As he spoke there was the sound of fire appliances approaching the burning cottage; someone in this wilderness must have seen it and alerted them. They were walking across fields for some time when they heard a car start up down stream on the other side of the river; 'I'll bet that's Murphy making his getaway, he won't get away with it he is now on the run.' They finally came out on to a country road near a couple of houses; Cooper noticed telephone wires going to both of them. He knocked loudly on the door of the first one and an angry man stuck his head out of a bedroom window; 'what the hell time do you call this, disturbing folk in the middle of the night.'

Cooper drew his Warrant card and said 'Police, can I use your phone sir?' There has been a fire at Marshman's cottage.

The man withdrew his head and they heard him coming down the stairs; after drawing several bolts and unlocking two locks he opened the door and let them in.

'I see you have some good security sir,' said Cooper dryly; 'could you show me where the phone is please?' He got onto the station and the Desk Sergeant promised to send a police vehicle to collect them, 'whereabouts are you,' he said; Cooper replied, 'that's a good question, just a minute and I'll ask.'

By now the man's wife had come down in her 'nightie,' she was also wearing a hair net and she had a kind heart, as seeing the state they were in she insisted on making them a cup of tea; it was very welcome. An hour later a 'paddy wagon' arrived to collect them; the driver apologized, 'Never mind,' said Cooper; 'it will be a novel experience for all of us.'

117

CHAPTER THIRTY TWO

Murphy drove north; he knew that the authorities would have put a full alert out for him so he would not be able to use conventional means of leaving the country. He had also had to leave the kayak behind, which he could have used to cross to one of the islands off Scotland. He had given up on the contract; now it was a case of saving his own skin, Millington Smythe would have to sort his own problems out. He had done his best, but things had been against him from the start and now he was on the run. Dawn was just coming up as he crossed the border into Scotland; he headed for Glasgow and had a bite to eat in a café in the centre of town before resuming his journey. He was making for the Kyle of Lochalsh where he could dump the car and catch the Skye ferry. By mid afternoon he had reached Fort William, after buying sandwiches and taking on more petrol he headed out on the road to Invergarrie. He hoped to reach Skye before nightfall and chafed at the twisting highland roads with their constant lay byes. Before catching the ferry he took the Beretta from the pack together with a couple of magazine clips of .22 ammo then he drove the car up to the headland and with the aid of a large stone on the accelerator sent it hurtling over the cliff into the sea. He caught the ferry to

Skye and got on the bus to Dunvegin which lay on the other side of the island.

It was dark when he arrived in the little fishing village, but he knew the place and headed for the Hotel. As he entered the bar through the haze of smoke he spotted the man he was looking for; it was Dougie McNab a big red faced fellow with an iron grey beard.

'Why if it isn'i ma old friend Shaun,' he bellowed, 'what brings ye to Skye; will ye have a wee dram?'

Shaun and Dougie went way back; having been involved in gun running to the Provos and other nefarious schemes that paid well.

Dougie caught his hand in a vice like grip and shook it warmly; 'Och man it does me old heart giud te see ye again, it's been gae quiet roond here since we parted.'

He shouted to the man behind the bar, 'twa' o' the same Jamie; come awa over here where we can hear oorselves bleather,' he put his arm round Shaun's shoulder and steered him to a table in the corner.

The drinks arrived and Dougie raised his glass, 'Slancha and may your shadow ne're grow less.'

He dropped his voice and murmured, 'ah hear you're in a spot o bother Shaun, can I help ye?'

The fact that Dougie knew he was on the run surprised Shaun, seemingly bad news travels fast.

'I was hopin' that you could help me to get to the ould country Dougie, things are a bit hot and I've outstayed me welcome in England.'

Dougie sipped his whisky and said slowly; 'have ye got enough money for diesel; normally ah would'ne ask ye, but the fishin' has been bad due to the weather this last three months.

'How much would you need to get to Mayo and back,' asked Shaun?'

'Aboot fifty ah' reckon.' mused Dougie.

'I'll have to draw a bankers draft from the local bank tomorrow,' said Shaun, 'when can we sail?'

'Tomorrow forenoon's high tide, we can be ready once the fuel is on board'

They had another couple of drinks and then headed for Dougie's cottage; his wife had died some years previously so he lived on his own. He unlocked the door and a Border collie rushed up to greet him; 'get doon ye'll have me over,' he bent down and coaxed the dog that gave his hand a lick and dashed inside. 'Daft dog,' he said affectionately, 'will ye mind sleepin' on yonder settle Shaun ah'll get ye some blankets.' He bustled about and made up a rough bed then produced a bottle of single malt whisky; pouring out two generous measures he handed one to Shaun, 'one for the road,' he said raising his glass.

CHAPTER THIRTY THREE

Cooper was preparing his report for the Public Prosecutors office; with the new photographic evidence linking the three men together he considered that he could present a good case against Millington Smythe, at the very least guilt by association. The body of PC Alec Wendling had been recovered from the river Yare and a warrant had been issued for the apprehension of Shaun Murphy on a murder charge. Bullet had been found lying on the river bank waiting for his master's return; he was taken back to the dog pound to await a new handler. Mollie and Sheila were now in a new safe house in Norwich and Cooper kept in touch by phone, he realized that Murphy must have followed him to every change of venue. There had been no reports of sightings of Murphy since the night of the attack, the trail it seemed had gone cold. All ports, airports and train stations had pictures of Murphy, but unfortunately they were not recent and in any case he had been wearing his disguise until he had reached Scotland.

'He's got to be stopped before he reaches Ireland;' Cooper was saying to his squad, 'otherwise he will be over the border and we can say goodbye; extradition to England from there is to say the least unreliable' The kayak that had been recovered after the attack on Marsh

121

man's Cottage had yielded little useful information, Murphy had obviously been wearing gloves during the attempted hit.

Foley was sent to find where Murphy had purchased it from and quickly found the Army and Navy store, the proprietor remembered it was bought by an Irishman, but his description was of a tall man with blonde hair and a mustache. 'No wonder no one has seen him,' said Cooper angrily, 'all the posters show a picture of his normal appearance.' A vision of the beige car and the blonde guy with dark glasses came in to his mind and he wished the ground would swallow him up. He had seen Murphy's change of appearance and hadn't acted on it; he had wasted police time. He notified Superintendent Trafford of the fresh evidence of Murphy's disguise and the pictures were replaced, but it had lost them valuable time.

However it produced two reports of sightings in Scotland, a café proprietor in Glasgow and a bus conductor on Skye. This was followed up by police forces in Scotland, but they had drawn a blank, the trail had gone cold in Skye.

CHAPTER THIRTYFOUR

The old fishing boat was taking a beating as she rounded the Northern coastline of Ireland, the Atlantic rollers swept over her decks and smashed against the wheelhouse and the wind flung spray caked her superstructure with salt spume. She rolled and plunged like a harpooned whale, her propeller racing as the stern came out of the water. It was blowing a force eleven gale and Mc.Nab fought with the wheel to keep her on course. He yelled above the roaring of the wind, 'I dinna ken when I've seen a worse one Shaun in all ma days at sea.' Shaun was a delicate shade of green and definitely not feeling well; he was usually a good sailor, but this storm was testing his ability to withstand the rigours of the ocean. He hung on to the rail inside the wheelhouse and braced himself against the motion of the boat; when they had left Dunvegin it had been relatively calm, but this storm had hit them suddenly and now they were fighting for their lives.

Dougie was trying to keep her heading into the waves, but the wind was blowing across the boat and taking her towards the coast. Shaun could see the lights of Londonderry through the sheets of rain; they were being driven towards the shore.

'Can you stop her drifting inshore Dougie, we're getting' awful close,' shouted Shaun.

Dougie shook his head, 'I have the engine flat oot, but the old girl has nay any more to give.' Just then a huge wave came over the bow and hit the reinforced glass on the wheelhouse and shattered it filling the place with icy green water; at the same time the engine stopped. Shaun managed to scramble to his feet, the wave had driven the wind out of him, he looked around for Dougie, but he was gone. Now the sea had the boat in its teeth and was driving it straight towards land; he managed to find a spare life jacket and put it on. Poor Dougie had been a sacrifice to the sea that he had loved all his life and now it had literally taken him to its bosom.

The lights of Derry were now mighty close as was the sound of the surf, then a miracle occurred, the wind suddenly dropped and the boat ran aground. He was still about twenty meters away from the shore, but unhesitatingly he dived overboard and struck out for the beach. The undertow snatched him twice as he neared the shoreline and he was exhausted when he finally managed to stand and wade out of the water. He fell to the sand his lungs burning with his exertions and he lay there for what seemed an age. The wind sprang up again and there was a terrible sound as the boat was swept by the incoming waves onto the nearby rocks and smashed to matchwood. He removed the life jacket and buried it in the sand, and then he squeezed as much water out of his clothing as he could. Turning towards the city he began to walk quickly away from the beach, he didn't want to be there when the wreck was discovered. He knew Derry well; he had done business there with the Provos and the Brits, he made his way to the Municipal Baths and went down to the boiler house, removing his outer garments he arranged them around the boiler and warmed himself while they dried. Mc.Fee the boiler man was probably round at the pub; he would give him something to stop his mouth when he came back. He had taken the precaution of wrapping his wallet in an oilskin bag before setting out in case he had to swim ashore, so at least his money was dry.

The warmth permeated his body and he fell asleep; 'what the hell d'ye call this,' the voice was familiar.
He opened his eyes and perceived Mc Fee holding a shovel and looking belligerent.

'Calm down Michael, don't ye know me, it's Shaun Murphy and I'm dryin' out after fallin' in the river.'
The old man squinted uncertainly in the half light, and then a toothy grin spread across his ruddy face.

'Why if it isn't Shaun; Mother of God, but ye surely put the wind up me,' he paused looking puzzled and said,' why did ye fall in the river?'

'Someone pushed me,' said Shaun, 'so I thought of me old friend Michael and here I am dryin' out.'

The smile on the man's face began to fade; 'sure now there's no one chasin' ye is there Shaun, I don't think I'd like to get involved in anythin' nasty like.'

'Ah Michael, sure there's nothin' like that, it was an accident; here's somethin' for your trouble, I'll be on me way soon onyway.'

The man palmed the money and the smile returned, 'take as long as ye like Shaun I have to go out me self as it happens.'

He scuttled up the stairs and out of the door presumably to renew his acquaintance with a glass of Porter.

When his clothes were reasonably dry he put them on and walked down to the bus station, the last bus to Sligo was due

in an hour. He bought a single ticket and sat down to wait, eventually the elderly bus came in and the passengers disembarked. He chose a seat at the back away from the windows and settled down behind a newspaper, the bus was filling up with the usual late evening crowd, some the worse for drink. An authoritative voice cut across the hubbub;
'Keep your seats please; my men will be coming round to check your documentation before the bus leaves.' It was the B Specials; Shaun's blood ran cold; keep calm now, he reached into his pocket and took the passport out and keeping the paper in front of his face held it out.

He heard the footsteps coming nearer the passport was taken and scrutinized; then it was handed back and the policeman moved on. What luck, he supposed that this was just routine and they were not looking for anyone in particular. When they left the bus started up and lurched out of the bus station; on the road it gradually picked up speed and began the journey to Sligo. It was a long journey and he slept a lot of the time, he would stop over in a motel and get a taxi home in the morning as Mary was staying with her mother.

CHAPTER THIRTY FIVE

Millington Smythe looked at the letter on his desk; it bore the crest of the Ministry of Justice. He opened it with trembling fingers and read the text, it was couched in civil tones, but the thrust of the letter left no room for misunderstanding. He was being invited to attend a hearing to answer charges regarding certain events in Norfolk and elsewhere connected with the unlawful killing of persons listed.

Putting down the letter he reached for the phone and rang his lawyer, 'Hallo James it's Millington Smythe here; could you spare me an hour of your time, something unexpected has come up and I need your advice?'

They met in his club near the Bank of England where in better days he had liked to hobnob with powerful investment bankers. He handed the letter over for Sir James Howard's opinion; he read it in silence and then looked over his steel rimmed glasses.

'You had better tell me the whole story,' he said, 'so we can find out at the hearing just what they have got.'

As Millington Smythe recounted the events that had led up to the murders Sir James held up his hand and asked, 'can you tell me if you were involved in the killings directly?'

'No of course not, in fact I tried to stop him by sending someone to …,'here he stopped realizing what he had just admitted to.

Sir James looked at him over his half glasses again and whispered, 'I didn't hear that and I suggest you forget that you said it otherwise you will condemn yourself out of your own mouth.' 'The main thing at this stage is to assess their evidence and then implement a damage limitation exercise.' 'Under no circumstances must you admit anything, they haven't got much otherwise they would have already charged you.' Leave it with me and I will reply to their letter; take some time off man you look terrible, are you sleeping properly?' After a few words of encouragement and telling him not to worry Sir James took his leave and Millington

Smythe ordered another brandy.

CHAPTER THIRTY SIX

Murphy left the small commercial hotel next morning and took a taxi home; he would arrive early and be waiting when Mary came home from her mother's. It was a typical Mayo day; overcast and raining and as he arrived outside his farmhouse he could see the mist spilling over the Ox Mountains. Murphy let himself in and made a cup of coffee, the place seemed depressing without Mary and his dog; still she shouldn't be long now.

He heard a car pull up outside; that must be her now; he opened the front door and went outside. A black car was drawn up at the gate and two men were getting out; he didn't recognize either of them, but instinctively he knew what they were!

The taller one called out, 'Hello there Shaun, I'm glad to see you're at home, it saves us a lot of time.'
Both pulled out guns as they approached him, he raised his hands and the second man searched him.

'What's this all about lads,' he said, 'I think you must have made a mistake, you know the work I've done for the Cause.'

The tall man smiled, 'you're the one that has made the mistake Shaun, by playin' both sides against the middle.'

129

'I've no idea what you're talkin about,' said Murphy, 'can't we go inside and discuss it?'

He thought of the Beretta nestling in his jacket, there might be a chance if they went inside.

'No Shaun there isn't the time, at least not for you; we have written evidence from the Brits that you have been givin' them information that cost good Catholic lives, so it's time to pay.'

Shaun began to laugh; the irony of the situation hit him like a blow; everything he had endured whilst he was on the run, the terrible storm which had deprived him of one of the best friends he had known, the stress of knowing that he could be apprehended at any moment, the realization that he would never see Mary again. Then the final irony, because they couldn't reach him here the British authorities had ensured that the I.R.A would do their work for them!

He was still laughing as they gunned him down and left him lying on the path, his sightless eyes looking up at the uncaring rain as it fell. Mary's taxi arrived an hour later and the old dog jumped out first, ran to his master and began licking his face, Mary got out and saw his body lying on the path, she gave a cry of anguish and ran to his side, throwing herself onto her knees she cradled his head in her arms; she kept saying over and over,

'I told you not to go, I told you Shaun.'

The taxi driver came and gently raised her up and took her into the house, sitting her down he went to the phone.

Outside the rain continued to fall on the silent tableau of a dead man and his dog.

CHAPTER THIRTY SEVEN

Cooper read the copy of the letter from Millington Smythe's solicitor; it was much as he had expected.

'My client will be attending the hearing set for the twenty fourth of May together with his barrister Sir James Howard QC. to repudiate allegations made against him.' 'He will fight to clear his name and bring charges against those who have instigated them.' It continued in this vein for three pages and Cooper threw the letter on the desk in disgust; the nerve of the guy.'

A report had come through from the local Garda in Mayo that Murphy had been the victim of an IRA hit and the case was under investigation. So that was another major player out of the picture, thought Cooper, 'he who lives by the sword etc.' Munro had been recalled to Scotland Yard: Cooper suspected that the 'Super' could have had a hand in that due to the man's incompetence.

He felt that there was enough evidence now to proceed with a conviction providing they could convince the presiding judge. He had heard of Sir James; who had not? The man was a legend in his lifetime and had successfully defended several large companies in well publicized cases. Still Crown Oil could afford the best, even though their share value had been dropping of late. When he thought of the killings and the trail of mayhem running through this case he felt angry that a few greedy men could wreak such destruction on ordinary people's lives. He found his thoughts turning to Sheila, due to pressure of work he had not had the opportunity to see her and determined to go the next day.

He parked outside the row of terrace houses in one of the streets that ran at the back of the Norfolk and Norwich Hospital. He had chosen the place because of its anonymity and heavily populated situation, it would be a very brave or reckless assassin that would attempt a hit here. Molly let him in and he went through to the back room where he found Sheila sitting looking out of the window at the small back garden.

She looked round and her face lit up, 'Hello stranger, I thought you had forgotten me,' she smiled and held out her hands.

He squeezed them and said, 'sorry. I've been so neglectful, but at least we seem to be coming in to the home straight now.'

'You mean I'll be able to rejoin the human race soon,' she said, teasing him.

'Well not quite yet,' but once we have a prosecution, and then things should get back to normal.'

'I thought you might like a trip out somewhere that is if Molly doesn't object?'

He drove over to Horning and they had lunch at the Swan, she was delighted that she could see the passing boats from the windows.

'This is where it all started,' he said, 'I began to get a handle on the case here after talking to a boat builder just up the road.

'Do you mind if we don't talk about it,' she said, it all seems like a never ending nightmare at the moment.'
'I'm sorry you will have to forgive me, the job is all I have to think about since my wife left me, I suppose one could call it an obsession.'

She lent her elbows on the table, cupped her face in her hands and looked long and hard into his eyes.
'You don't have to be on your own you know,' she said.
He reached across the table and took her hands in his; 'have you really thought what you would be letting yourself in for,' he said gently, 'that's what choked Angela off, she got tired of the uncertain hours the missed meals, not knowing where I was, and the lack of a social life.'
'It isn't fair on a woman to have to put up with that day in and day out.' She withdrew her hands and looked down at the table cloth; 'so you don't think I could cope, you don't know me very well Dan, I spent my childhood mostly alone and have lived alone up till now without cracking up.' 'It's just knowing that you could care for me; that would make everything all right, I know I could put up with all the rest.' Cooper was deeply moved at her response, 'don't think that I haven't similar feelings Sheila, but until this case is over you are still in danger and it's my responsibility to see that you come to no harm. 'I'm sure that we can work it all out when we have more time together to discuss it, now I had better get you back to the Bastille.'

CHAPTER THIRTY EIGHT

The meeting of the Board had not gone well; give him his due Bowker had gone in to bat for him, but the rest of the directors were losing their nerve in the light of present developments and wanted a scapegoat. Shares had lost thirty percent of their value since the hearing had been announced and were still heading downwards. Millington Smythe drove back to his house in Surbiton wondering how he was going to break the news to Greta. Things had not been right between them since the onset of this business and he suspected that what he had to tell her would be the last straw. As he pulled into the drive her BMW flashed past on the way out; there was a man in the passenger seat that looked familiar. It was the tennis coach from her club; he had been introduced to him at one of the functions they had attended there. He had not liked the fellow from the first with his oily black hair and over familiar manner and now his worst fears looked as if they were being realized, she had left him. Disconsolately he parked the Bentley and he let himself into the house, he went upstairs to the master bedroom and saw the signs of a hasty departure; the drawers of her dressing table had been emptied and there were gaps in the huge range of dresses in the wardrobe. There was a hastily scribbled message on her mirror written in lipstick,

'You had your chance and you blew it, I shall be sending for the rest of my things and you will be hearing from my solicitors in due course.' He sat heavily down on the bed and buried his head in his hands, 'God when will this end,' he moaned rocking back and forth. He eventually went downstairs and opened the drinks cabinet then he spent the next few hours getting paralytic and awoke shivering with cold on the marble floor of the conservatory next morning

He felt as if he had a trip hammer going full blast in his head and endeavored to shave himself ending up cutting himself several times and went downstairs with pieces of toilet paper stuck to his face. He rang in and told his secretary that he had the flu and would be unable to come in. There was a knock at the door; Blast! Who the devil could this be, forgetting his appearance he opened the door and saw two diminutive persons clutching copies of a religious missive.

'Have you considered how God feels about you?' one inquired earnestly.

Millington Smythe saw red, 'I can bloody well tell you what I think about Him and silly sods like you; going around pestering people with your half baked notions.'

'I'll tell you about God, He couldn't give a toss about you, me or anyone else; you're on your own in this world and there isn't a next one, so bugger off and bother someone else.'

He slammed the door and lurched off towards the drinks cabinet.

CHAPTER THIRTY NINE

'It's a pity we haven't a bit more evidence to definitely tie the Chairman into the killings,' said Trafford, 'mostly it is by association rather that direct.'
Cooper nodded, 'the trouble is sir that the only other people that could provide that evidence are dead.'
'Which leaves us with little room for maneuver, the best we can hope for is guilt by association.'
'It would help if we could find the facility that Duffy was released from,' said Cooper. 'I think it's time to contact Sir Perry Warnes again, he has access to the records of the military and there must be some information as to where Duffy was detained.'
Trafford agreed, 'get onto it Cooper I think you could be on the right track, now if you will excuse me I have a function to attend.'

'Hello Detective sergeant Cooper, nice to hear from you again, what can I do for you?'
The bustling business like voice of Sir Perry Warnes was warm and friendly and Cooper explained the reason that he was calling.
There was a slight pause before Sir Perry responded, 'hmn, that could be a bit of a problem, you see the War

Department are reluctant to reveal information regarding these places, mainly to do with the privacy of the individual involved and security of the facility.'

Why was he being evasive,? Cooper was immediately suspicious and pressed the Minister further.

'Surely sir the fact that this could be vital information regarding a conspiracy to release this man overrides other considerations?

'Well I'll see what I can do, but when it comes to National Security matters my hands are tied.'

Despite Cooper's insistence Sir Perry was adamant that he could do little to help and that it would take a decision at Parliamentary level to change things. Cooper rang off feeling frustrated and also that he had run into that tenuous wall of silence that seemed to pervade the halls of power when figures of authority didn't want to answer awkward questions.

He was going to have to circumvent this obstacle somehow if he was going to glean information regarding Crown Oil's involvement.

Foley supplied the answer during a conversation they were having about the case, 'surely Sergeant there's a chance that Duffy was not in a military psychiatric unit, but one perhaps in the private sector?' 'Possibly it might even be a subsidiary business owned by Crown Oil, you could have a look through the Business Register.'

'Better still Foley; as it was your idea I'll let you have the honour of plowing through the register, I have to go out and visit our Witness Protection subject.'

'Oh; that's not fair sergeant,' Foley said with feeling.

Cooper grinned, 'no it's not fair Foley, its called delegation, something that you will need when you

become a D.I. some day,' with that he picked up his raincoat and headed for the door.
'I bet I know who'll get the credit for it though,' muttered Foley as he rang the Library.

CHAPTER FORTY

The court room was packed with interested parties, shareholders, the Press and rubbernecks who had come to see one of the 'Fat Cats' get his comeuppance. There were also representatives from companies that had a vested interest in the possible downfall of Crown Oil, the sharks were gathering for a possible feeding frenzy. The presiding judge was His Honour Sir Hector Playford , a no nonsense figure well versed in cases of commercial misconduct. Millington Smythe was sitting with his brief as this was a preliminary hearing; he looked terrible and appeared to have aged overnight. He fiddled nervously with his spectacle case and seemed to be having difficulty in concentrating when spoken to. Sir James Howard was struggling to keep the man focused on what he was saying.

You must try and concentrate on the advice I am giving you, once you start giving evidence you will be on your own 'Under no circumstances admit to anything connected with the case and do not make any speculative statements. 'Leave the final summary to me at the end of your interrogation, I will by then know exactly what we are up against; and for goodness sake pull yourself together.'

Sir Hector opened proceedings by outlining the terms of the hearing, stressing that it was to determine whether there was a case to answer, in which case the matter would then be referred to a Criminal court. Crown Prosecution's evidence would be presented and then could be challenged by the defending advocate. The hearing got under way by the Crown calling for Detective Sergeant Cooper to present his evidence. He outlined the case against Duffy, producing photographic and forensic evidence; he then turned to Nicholson's involvement, linking the two men by the photos of the attack in Abundu and the connection with Crown Oil through the bank statements he had recovered from Nicholson's office. Then he produced the photograph of the unit in Yemen containing pictures of the two men together with their C.O. Millington Smythe.

Rising unsteadily to his feet Millington Smythe made an effort to gather himself; 'my Lord I deny the assumption that I had anything to do with this terrible business, I am a responsible servant of a reputable company and also served my country without a blemish on my character.' 'I freely admit that these men served under me during their term in Aden, but I deny any association with them after leaving the service.' I have been under considerable strain since this matter arose and will fight these ridiculous charges through the courts till I have cleared my good name.' At a sign from his brief he sat down mopping his brow, he was sweating profusely. Sir James Howard rose to his feet and holding the lapels of his gown proceeded to sum up. 'Having heard the evidence from the Crown prosecution I find it hard to understand why they have decided to bring it to this hearing.' 'It is painfully obvious that despite all the photographs, bank accounts and what have you, they have utterly failed to prove a connection between these men and my client other than that of being in the Army together.' 'To say the least the connection is tenuous and certainly does not prove that my client played any part in these recent criminal activities.' 'We shall of course be pursuing this matter through the courts in order to restore my client's character and to extract suitable damages from those responsible for bringing these charges.'

After Sir Robert's rebuttal of the State's evidence the judge began his summing up. 'I must compliment Detective Sergeant Cooper on his presentation of the evidence and his obvious dedication in the pursuit of this case; however there is no doubt that at best it only shows a connection between the plaintive and the other two men.' 'Learned council has put his finger firmly on the fact that if there is any charge brought against his client it would be difficult to prove conclusively any guilt on his part.' 'Therefore to avoid any further action in this matter I must set it aside unless or until further evidence can be produced which clearly links him to the crimes committed in this case; I have no choice but to declare this hearing closed and the plaintiff is discharged without a stain on his character..'

The look of relief on Millington Smythe's face was startling; he seemed to shed years of ageing as the judge discharged him. He shook Sir Robert's hand until his brief had to disengage it, then drawing himself up to his full height he glared at Cooper and turning on his heel walked out of the court. The detective was devastated; all that work and sacrifice had just been thrown away like an old garment, not only that, but that bastard would be in a position to sue the pants off the Police.' Not wishing to run the gauntlet of the Press he left the building by the back entrance, Millington

141

Smythe on the other hand was basking in the publicity whilst he regaled the Media from the steps of the courthouse.'

'I shall not rest until this gross deformation of my character has been refuted through the courts and I shall be seeking the maximum amount in damages against the police for bringing these unfounded accusations against me.'

Sir Robert stopped him in full flight saying to the Press that his client would be taking a short break whilst he considered his options.

As he hustled Millington Smythe down to the waiting limmo he hissed in his client's ear, 'you would be well advised to keep a low profile for the time being; that policeman has not finished with you yet and will redouble his efforts to discover further evidence.'

'I recommend that you wait awhile before going ahead with litigation, otherwise it could rebound on you.'

Full of euphoria Millington Smythe ignored his brief's warning and instructed his solicitors to commence proceedings against the Metropolitan and Norfolk police forces. He would show the world and Greta that he was not a man to be trifled with, he would have his revenge in court and he had certainly not finished with her either.'

There were celebrations in Crown Oil's boardroom at the outcome of the case and even Millington Smith's adversaries at the last meeting came over to congratulate him. The company's shares had bounced back to their best value and he had been reinstated without objection. Bowker waxed almost lyrical in his fulsome praise of the Chairman; extolling his loyalty to the Company and his untiring efforts on their behalf. The object of his unstinting praise stood basking in this unsolicited testimonial to his excellence savoring every glowing word.

CHAPTER FORTY ONE

It was a totally different picture in Cooper's office; he sat at his desk feeling that his world had been turned upside down. Chief Superintendent Trafford said little during their meeting after the hearing; 'I made the final decision Cooper after reading the evidence, so I must take responsibility for the outcome.'

The papers had been full of Millington Smyth's triumphalism on the courthouse steps and his threats of litigation against the Police.

Foley breezed into the office bearing copious notes from his spell at the Library, Cooper looked up; 'I hope you've got some good news for me Foley, it's been nothing but doom and gloom up to now.'

'The stuff I have here could wipe the smirk off Millington Smythe's face sergeant, look at this.'

He extracted a sheet from the pile and showed him, the heading was of a private Nursing Home called 'Perrivale and underneath was a list of the Directors and Medical Staff.

As he looked at it Cooper's heart gave a leap, the first two were Sir Perry Warnes and Millington Smythe. The Chief Psychologist was a certain Dr. Stanislous Podolski with a string of letters after his name too numerous to take in.

This was pure gold; it was obviously where Duffy had absconded from and was the reason why Sir Perry had been so evasive.

'Well done Foley, this could be the connection we have been looking for; you have excelled yourself this time.'

'Where is this place,' said Cooper, 'anywhere near here?'

'Essex,' responded Foley, 'near Clacton according to the map, I've got the co-ordinates here.'

'Well in that case I think we should give them a look,' said Cooper, 'come on you've earned your keep this week.'

Soon they were speeding down the A140 heading for Ipswich; Foley wound down the window he couldn't abide that awful tobacco Cooper smoked.

It took them two and a half hours to reach the small hamlet outside Clacton where the Nursing Home was situated.

Cooper swept through the entrance gates and down the leafy driveway to an imposing building standing in large mature grounds.

Parking the car in the official car park outside the front door he got out and beckoned Foley to follow him. The entrance hall was large and airy; as he looked around Cooper noticed that the décor was in soft pastel colours, presumably so as not to upset the inmates. A severe looking woman in her fifties wearing a nurse's uniform looked up and asked Cooper if she could help him.

I hope so,' he said showing his Warrant Card,

'I would like a word with Dr. Podolski.'

'I'm afraid he is not back from lunch yet Detective Cooper,' she said.

'Detective Sergeant,' he corrected her, 'never mind we'll wait,' he walked over to a row of chairs and sat down.

After a quarter of an hour a rotund little man came through the door looking cross; 'dere iss a strange car in my space Rachael, do you know who's it iss?'

The woman indicated Cooper who stood up and extended his hand, 'Detective Sergeant Cooper Doctor, I'm sorry if I have taken your space, but I was anxious to see you.'

Podolski frowned, 'I vish you had phoned before coming; I have a very busy schedule and normally only see people by appointment.'

Cooper smiled broadly; 'I appreciate that you are a busy man Doctor, but so am I and Police business will not wait for anyone.' 'Is there somewhere that we can talk confidentially?' he asked, 'I have no wish to embarrass you.'

Something akin to fear showed momentarily in the man's eyes, but it vanished and he suddenly became charming.

'Of course, please come zis vay,' he ushered them into a large room with a desk placed in front of the window and a leather couch strategically situated at an angle across one side of the room; one of the walls was covered with medical books. There were a couple of chairs in front of the desk; his smile looked as if it had been painted on as he bade them to be seated.

Sitting behind his desk he placed the tips of his fingers together and said pleasantly, 'now how can I be of service to you Detective Sergeant.'

Cooper leaned forward confidentially and said, 'we are here to ask you about an ex patient of yours Doctor.'

'Oh, and who might zat be?" he was beginning to have difficulty in maintaining that artificial smile.

'Duffy,' said Cooper innocently.

146

The smile disappeared and Podolski started to sweat; 'I do not know who zat is, I have had no one of zat name here.'

'In that case you won't mind if I look through your records of recent patients Doctor Podolski.'

'Ah, I am sorry, but I cannot allow zat, zey are confidential, betveen me and my patients.'

'This is a murder inquiry Doctor and I am sure you would not wish to bc arrested for obstructing the police in the execution of their duty.'

Podolski stood up; 'I vish to have my solicitor present.'

'In that case sir we will continue this conversation at my headquarters where you will be allowed to contact him, what's it to be?'

Podolski pulled out a handkerchief and began to mop his brow; he was cornered and decided on self preservation.

He picked up the phone and rang his receptionist; 'could you bring ze Patient List in please Rachael.'

There was a knock at the door and the woman came in and laid a buff coloured file on the desk.

Cooper picked it up and began to look through it.

'It vasn't my fault you understand, he got out during ze night after overpowering one of ze male nurses,' Podolski's voice was beginning to become shrill.

There it was; Duffy's details, when he arrived at the place, but nothing about his disappearance.

Cooper looked Podolski in the eyes and murmured, 'If it was not your fault why did you not report it Doctor?'

'The man was a homicidal maniac; you must have known what he was capable of and by not reporting his escape you have become an accessory to murder.'

The man held his head in his hands and started to sob, Cooper stood up and began to read him his rights, then coming round the desk he handcuffed him. Between them they lifted Podolski out of his chair and took him out into the hallway, as they passed the gaping receptionist Cooper commented, 'he has been arrested and will be going to Norwich to face charges, good day Rachael.'

CHAPTER FORTY TWO

Millington Smythe sat at his desk dictating a letter to his secretary, he was happy and his star was in the ascendancy once more; he had been speaking to his solicitor this morning who assured him that the preparation of the case against the police was progressing apace.

His phone rang and he picked it up and said heartily, 'hello 'Millington Smythe speaking,' his secretary watched his face as it went from carefree to ashen in a millisecond.

He listened in stunned silence as the caller spoke, finally putting down the phone with trembling hand.

'Are you all right sir,' the secretary inquired concernedly, 'can I get you a coffee or something stronger?' by now he had turned a pale shade of gray.'

Without replying he stood up and staggered out of the room; she followed him as far as the door to the executive washroom; as he entered she went for help.

The call had been from an agitated Sir Perry Warnes who had just been informed of the arrest of Podolski.

Things seemed to be coming unglued big time and the phones amongst those involved became red hot as the day progressed.

The Chairman went home early and began to pack; he wasn't going to await a visitation from the police; it was self preservation time. He opened the wall safe and removed what money there was and any incriminating papers, which he duly burned in the fireplace. Then stuffing his flight bag with clothing and pocketing his passport he went out to the Bentley and headed for Heathrow, there was no extradition treaty with Brazil.

As the Boing 707 lifted off the tarmac and began its climb out the police had arrived at his house to find that the bird had flown. They saw the door of the wall safe open and all it's contents gone; Cooper noticed the charred ashes in the fireplace and guessed there would not be much to find in the way of incriminating evidence. A nation wide search was instituted, but when Millington Smythe's Bentley was found parked in the long stay car park at London Airport it was clear he had left the country.

'He's scarpered to Brazil,' said Cooper bitterly, 'we have no extradition treaty with them so he's got away Scot free.'

'Can't we freeze his assets?' said Foley, 'he's fled the country to avoid arrest.

'That's already being looked into,' said Cooper, 'trouble is he may have funds abroad which he can draw on.'

'We shall just have to hope that Podolski is prepared to sing for his supper; come on Foley let's go down and see what we can get out of him.'

CHAPTER FORTY THREE

Ibn ben Doud read the news item with great interest; 'Chairman of Crown Oil Flees to Brazil,' shouted the bold headline. Sitting in his air conditioned office in central Aden he scanned the story eagerly; he was of Yemeni extraction and this man had led a raid on his tribe during hostilities back in 1956. It had resulted in most of his family being wiped out including his wife and children; he had sworn to avenge them, but had been unable to reach this man up till now.

'Allah be praised,' he said,' I shall be able to avenge my people by executing this infidel.'

He called through to his partner and showed him the newspaper, 'you must take care of the business till I return Ibrahim; this is Kismet my brother; I have been chosen to be the instrument of justice, Allah is great.'

He visited the Mosque to give thanks for this revelation and then booked a plane to Cairo where he caught an international flight to Rio de Janeiro.

As his plane sped on its way at 30,000 feet he reviewed his life; he had been blessed by Allah in having a quick brain and being successful in business; he had originally started work as a stevedore on the dockside of Aden as a young boy. He had shown considerable aptitude and being able to read and write was soon being employed in the lading office handling the documentation for the import and export business.

Saving his small surplus from a frugal lifestyle he eventually rented a small office in the business sector of Aden and opened up as an Import Export company. Knowing the shipping set up like the back of his hand he was able to make favorable deals with large companies and soon he had established himself at the forefront of his field.

Now he had been given the opportunity to revenge himself for his loss, Allah was good. Satisfied, he adjusted his seat and was soon sleeping like a baby. Some hours later he looked out of the window and caught his first glimpse of the giant statue of Jesus with his arms outstretched as the plane came in to land at Rio airport. After collecting his luggage from the carousel and clearing Customs he managed to get a taxi and to experience his first impressions of the city, to say it was bustling and colorful was an understatement, it hit you between the eyes like a hyperactive rainbow. The taxi pulled up outside his hotel, he paid off the driver and a page collected his luggage. Finally after signing in he was shown his room and thankfully slumped into a chair, he was beginning to experience jet lag.

CHAPTER FORTY FOUR

Once Podolski started to talk there was no stopping him; the thought of being charged as an accessory to murder had opened the floodgates. He still maintained that Duffy had got out without any help from the staff, but he confirmed that the man had been transferred to 'Perryvale' at Millington Smythe's request. He let slip that several celebrities had been treated for drug and alcohol problems at the clinic and it was also where various politicians met their mistresses. During the course of the interrogation Cooper pressed Podolski for information regarding Sir Perry Warne's involvement with the place.

'He und Millington Smythe vere ze founders of it;' insisted Podolski, 'zay bought ze house und turned it into a place vere top people could relax, vile it vos run as a clinic for rich persons as a cover.'

'Zay made a fortune from it over the years I tell you.'

'No doubt you didn't do too badly out of it yourself,' remarked Cooper dryly, 'so when Duffy disappeared you kept quiet knowing an investigation would uncover the real purpose of the place and your cosy little arrangement would be exposed.' Podolski nodded eagerly. 'Dat is right, all vould come crashing down and it vould make a big scandal.'

Cooper pushed a sheet of paper and a pen over to Podolski; 'now perhaps you would kindly put all that down on paper for me and I will see what I can do for you.' Podolski began to scribble frantically; Cooper turned to Foley; 'can you wait for him to finish and bring his statement up to me, I've got to make an urgent phone call?'

He left the interview room and went back to his office; picking up the phone he rang the Ministry of Defense and asked for Sir Perry. He was told that the minister was unavailable; I bet he is, thought Cooper putting down the phone; probably tendering his resignation to the PM at this very moment. Foley came up with the signed statement and Cooper rang Chief Superintendent Trafford, picking up the statement he winked at Foley and went upstairs. The papers next day were full of the sudden resignation of Sir Perry, the reason given was illness due to pressure of work and the PM had 'accepted it with regret,' the minister would be retiring to the family home in the Cotswolds to grow roses.

'Isn't it wonderful Foley what our masters can achieve from a failed career, if it had been you or me we would have finished up in the 'slammer.'

It's the way of the world I'm afraid Guv,' said Foley sagely, 'do you fancy a cup of tea?'

154

CHAPTER FORTY FIVE

After spending two weeks in a cockroach ridden hotel in down town Rio Millington Smythe decided he'd had enough of keeping a low profile. Anonymity was one thing, but living in squalor was not for the likes of him; so he decided to find something more in keeping with the kind of surroundings he was accustomed to. Before leaving England he had called into his bank and withdrawn as much money as he was allowed, which he hid in the false bottom of a suitcase. On arrival in Rio he had opened an account in the name of Gardener, which had been his mother's maiden name. Next he hired a taxi for the day and spent time looking in the more affluent suburbs of Rio for a suitable let. He finally settled on a whitewashed single story casa in a walled garden, which was situated in a quiet leafy road three miles from the center of the city. The rent was very reasonable as it was owned by a once well to do family who had fallen on hard times and were glad to let it out. It was fully furnished and he moved in the next day with much relief after quitting his previous accommodation. At first he hardly ventured out during the day, taking a stroll down the street and back again at night; however as time passed he became bolder and took to walking down to a small coffee house nearer the city.

It was here that he met a talkative young man by the name of Antonio O'Mally, who was the product of an unlikely union between an Irish deckhand and a local girl. What Millington Smythe did not know was that Antonio was a freelance photographer; one of the many streetwise beings in Rio who scraped a precarious living by picking up information and capitalizing on it. Antonio had recently been witness to the abduction of a suspected Nazi by Mossad and the pictures he had taken had been circulated round the world by Reuters. He was paid handsomely for them and had treated himself to a brand new Japanese camera with a zoom lens, which he carried with him wherever he went. Millington Smythe took to Antonio who made himself useful by providing information regarding life in this cosmopolitan country. He became Millington Smythe's 'gofer' for which service he was well paid; this suited the former as he did not care to be seen within the city. One thing he did not allow were photos of him, Antonio had tried on one occasion and had incurred Millington Smythe's intense displeasure.

CHAPTER FORTY SIX

Things had settled down so Cooper decided that Sheila could be released from surveillance and relocated to a place of her own choosing. The school in Swindon had long since replaced her so there would be the need for her to find a new post wherever she decided to put down her roots.

He discussed it with her during a meal they had together in a small country restaurant, 'have you decided where you would like to relocate?' he asked her.

She looked across the table at him and said, 'I haven't come to any definite conclusion yet Dan, what do you think?'

'Well, do you think you could stand living here in Norfolk, it's a great place to live and there are lot's of schools if that's what you want to do.'

'I'm not sure,' she said slowly, 'so much has happened since the accident; I feel that I need a sea change, something totally different to teaching.'

'Say like keeping some 'Copper' warm at nights?' He grinned and reached across the table and held her hand.

'She laughed and said, 'is that your idea of a proposal or just an indecent suggestion?'

'Both,' he said and they burst out laughing.

He paid the bill and they went out to the car holding hands, as they reached the car he took her in his arms.

Next morning he came in late, Foley was taken aback somewhat as Cooper had a reputation for punctuality, 'morning boss,' he said, 'or should it be good afternoon.'
'Less of your lip Foley,' said Cooper grinning like a Cheshire cat, 'it's a good job I'm in a good mood otherwise you would be on crossing duty this morning.'
'May one ask to what we owe this merry mood sergeant?' said Foley ignoring the threat. 'You may Foley as you are going to be my Best Man next Saturday at the City Hall.'
'You have got another suit, rather than that one, which by the look of it you sleep in?' said Cooper to the now open mouthed Cadet.
'Oh; er, yes boss the one I save for funerals and other jollifications,' said Foley recovering.
'Well it's going to have a completely new experience next week, and so are you my lad.'
'Congratulations sarge; who's the unfortunate woman?'
Cooper raised his eyes to the ceiling in mock horror, 'where do they find these cheeky kids, the current generation have no respect.' 'To answer your impudent question it is no other that Sheila our victim of the Witness Protection Scheme.'
Foley looked genuinely pleased, 'I think you're a lucky man Sarge, many congrats once again; I'm really looking forward to giving you away.'
He ducked as Cooper hurled a file at his head. Things were getting back to normal once again and Cooper felt as if a weight had been lifted from his shoulders, not only because the Broadland killings had been resolved, but also because he

had met Sheila and she had consented to become his wife, knowing the drawbacks of being married to a policeman.

CHAPTER FORTY SEVEN

Finishing his prayers Ibn Ben Doud got up from his prayer mat, rolled it up and put it reverently in his flight bag. For the last two weeks he had haunted the coffee bars and showed the picture he had cut from the newspaper in Aden of Millington Smythe to anyone who would care to look. He also visited the Press buildings in the hope that someone had photographed him or knew his whereabouts without success. It was as if the man had vanished without trace, indeed he obviously wanted to be invisible to the authorities. Ibn Ben Doud began to realize the enormity of his undertaking and also that he would need professional help in order to achieve his goal. He asked at the reception desk of his hotel whether they could recommend someone and was given an address on the seamy side of Rio. He rang for a taxi and gave the driver the address, they drove across to an area that became more and more run down until the taxi stopped outside a building with a board proclaiming in Portuguese; 'International Detective Agency; missing wives found with great speed, reports also.

He entered the establishment which was quite dark inside and the only thing that seemed to be animated was the great rotating fan on the ceiling. However as his eyes adjusted to

160

the gloom he saw a large figure sitting behind a desk wearing a suit which he guessed had been white at some time in the very distant past. The man was grossly overweight and sweated profusely in the mid day heat;

'How may I be of service Senhoor?' he said brushing away a persistent fly with a pudgy hand. With growing misgivings Ibn Bin Doud explained his requirements; the man listened in silence until he had finished.

Then leaning forward and looking at him with little black close set eyes he asked, 'why do you wish to find this man Senhoor?'

Ibn Bin Doud was momentarily at a loss, however he rallied and told him that the man owed him money and had absconded without paying him. The man obviously did not believe him.

'It seems the sum owed must indeed be large for you to come all the way to Brazil to find him?'

Bin Doud lost it; 'do you want the commission or not, there are plenty of other detectives in Rio.'

'Please Senhoor there is no need for discord, I will be happy to help you, but I must ask these things otherwise I could have my license taken away by the policia.'

He extended his hand; 'my name is Jesus Da Silva and I am very successful at what I do; I shall require daily expenses and a fee on finding the man you seek. 'If you wish me to begin I shall require a photo of the man and his name; also details of why he is here in Rio.'

Ibn Bin Doud gave him the photo and provided the other details plus a weeks expenses,

'You may pay me in American Dollars or Reals as you wish, the sum for the week is thirty five Reals or sixteen Dollars.'

He paid Da Silva in Reals which he had brought with him.

He omitted to disclose the real reason for finding Millington Smythe guessing that the man did not wish to press the point. Da Silva stood up and shook him by the hand, the effort of escorting his client to the door brought him out in a fresh bout of sweating and he mopped his face with a grubby handkerchief. As he leant back in the seat of his taxi on the return journey to his hotel Bin Doud wondered if he had made the right choice of private eye, the man seemed focused, but he seemed in danger of initiating a heart attack when he moved around.

CHAPTER FORTY EIGHT

Cooper's 'Stag Night' was in full swing, the pub was full of 'Coppers,' in various stages of inebriation.

Ben weaved an uncertain path towards Cooper who was propping up the bar smoking innumerable roll ups, 'those things,'ll do for you one day Dan,' he said putting a large arm round Cooper's shoulders, 'how about a top up?'

He hailed the harassed barmaid, 'two pint's of bitter darlin, this man needs fortification,' indicating the bridegroom.

Molly was twisting the night away on the small dance floor with Foley; he was on ginger beer as he had been charged with getting Cooper home. Earlier in the evening the 'Super' had turned up and given a complimentary oration; wishing Dan every happiness in his forthcoming nuptials, then after a dry sherry he wisely departed.

There was the usual horseplay and several glasses got broken in the course of the celebration, but by and large everyone had a good time and it was a happy Cooper that was poured into the waiting police van. After what seemed like a lifetime of people saying their goodbyes Foley was able to pull away and drive his now insensible charge back to his flat. On arrival he then had the pantomime of getting

Cooper's door key from him; after he had slid giggling down the wall a couple of times Foley had to hold him up with one hand and grope in Cooper's pockets in order to retrieve the key. As he opened the front door Cooper passed him and burst into song as he made for the stairs. By now the lights in other flats in the complex were coming on and people were leaning out of the windows wondering what was going on. Foley wished the ground would open and swallow him; especially as Cooper had come back out again and was serenading the onlookers.

'Come on Sarge, let's get you to bed ,' said Foley desperately; Cooper drew himself up to his full height and said , 'I don't fancy you and besides I'm getting married to Sheila tomorrow ,' he then rounded things off by falling over backwards and bursting into uncontrollable laughter.

By the time Foley had got his wayward charge safely tucked in and snoring fit to bust, he was totally exhausted and reaching his digs made straight for his bed. Just before turning out the light he checked once more that the wedding ring was on his bedside cabinet.

CHAPTER FORTY NINE

Da Silva did the rounds of the cheaper hotels showing the picture of Millington Smythe; it was a very hot day and he was sweating more profusely that usual, consequently his suit became even more wrinkled that usual and there were damp patches under the arms and the middle of his back. He stopped at a small café and ordered a coffee, as he looked around the customers his gaze fell on a young man and a military looking person in his fifties. They were in earnest conversation and totally engrossed in whatever they were discussing, there was something familiar about the older man then it hit him, he was looking at Millington Smythe. He had altered his appearance by dyeing his hair and had shaved off his mustache, but to Da Silva's experienced eye there was no mistake. What a stroke of luck; he could have been searching for this man for months, however there was no hurry; as if he informed his client immediately the expenses would cease. He would find out where the man was living first and then tell Bin Doud in his own time; he drank his coffee, paid the bill and walked out of the café. Best not to let the target see him, it made following more difficult and besides he disliked unnecessary expenditure of energy.

There was a small park across the road from the café he crossed the road and sat on a bench where he could observe without being seen.

Taking out his handkerchief he mopped his brow once more, 'God it is hot,' he could feel the rivulets of sweat running down his chest and back.

Fifteen minutes later the couple came out of the café and after standing talking for a while the young man walked off towards the centre of town. Millington Smythe looked around the square before setting off in the opposite direction; he walked slowly keeping to the shady side of the street. Mopping his brow once more Da Silva heaved his great carcass up and began to follow at a discreet distance. They carried on through the outskirts of the city till Millington Smythe turned down a tree lined street.

Da Silva slipped into a gateway as his quarry turned to check that no one was following; satisfied he continued until he came to a gate in a high walled garden and let himself in. Cautiously the detective went to the gate and checked the number, he had already noted the street name, he wrote both into his notebook and turning made his way back from whence he had come. He was elated that he had made such a simple discovery of his victim's whereabouts and could inform his client at his leisure.

CHAPTER FIFTY

The day of Cooper's wedding to Sheila started with blue skies
and little cloud, Molly was helping Sheila into her dress at
the flat and was to be one of the witnesses at the civil
marriage ceremony at the City hall. The time of the service
was eleven thirty and the couple intended to honeymoon in
the Lake District

'Are you all packed Sheila?' called out Molly as she made
yet another cup of tea?

'Yes we are going to leave straight after the service,' she
said as she examined her seams.

'Aren't you going to stay for drinks after,' said Molly?

'I don't think my husband to be could face that after last
night's capers,' laughed Sheila, 'he is definitely feeling
fragile this morning.'

'So much so that he hasn't had a cigarette, so he must be
feeling pretty bad.'

The time came to depart for the wedding and an Austin
Princess Limousine purred up to the front door complete with
white ribbons draped across the bonnet. The two women
climbed aboard complete in all their finery and with a crowd
of onlookers waving them off they departed for City Hall.

Cooper was waiting in the Registrar's outer office looking decidedly peaky whilst Foley fidgeted nervously; constantly checking the ring in the inside pocket of his suit. There was a sprinkling of Cooper's colleagues hovering in the background to wish them well on departure and probably to douse them in confetti. Sheila and Molly arrived and the wedding party was ushered into the inner sanctum. The Registrar looked over his gold rimmed spectacles then opened the book and started the ceremony. When it came to the exchange of rings Foley in his haste managed to drop the ring on the floor and spent several embarrassing minutes trying to recover it. Finally they were able to continue and on completion sealed it with a kiss. Molly wept and was consoled by Ben as the newly weds ran down the steps of the City Hall through a barrage of confetti to Cooper's car.

As they pulled away there was a horrible sound of tin cans being dragged behind the car, rounding a bend Cooper nipped out and removed them, climbing back in he said, 'after last night I don't think I could put up with that racket all the way to Ambleside.'

He leaned across and kissed her, 'Hello Mrs. Cooper,' he said, 'Please keep your eyes on the road Dan,' she said as an oncoming driver swerved to avoid him. 'He raised his eyes heavenwards and groaned, 'we haven't been married five minutes and already she's nagging.'

She gave him a playful dig in the ribs, 'there, that's for making sarcastic comments.'

'Ouch, she's assaulting me as well; I should have brought my boxing gloves.'

'Whatever sort of honeymoon had you got in mind,' she said, 'I'm not an S.M. sort of girl!'

He shook his head in mock disappointment, 'no sense of adventure these modern women'. He turned onto the Kings Lynn Road and headed for the A1 and the North.

CHAPTER FIFTY ONE

It was three weeks before Da Silva informed Ibn Bin Doud that he had located Millington Smythe. He collected his fee as well as his expenses which were pretty generous and waddled out of the hotel leaving a very satisfied customer.
Bin Doud left the hotel and went to the local market and eventually found what he was looking for. A stall which sold curios and brick a brac provided the item he required; it was a large ceremonial dagger in a leather sheath. After some prolonged haggling he purchased it for ten Reals and returned to the hotel feeling elated. When he had completed his prayers he went out again and hailed a taxi, this time he was carrying the knife under his coat. He instructed the driver to drive around the area where his victim lived to familiarize himself with the layout. Satisfied he returned to the hotel and prepared himself for a return visit the following day, he had yet to see Millington Smythe for himself.

Next morning he set out to shadow his prey and if possible carry out his plan; he positioned himself where he could see the gate to the Casa. He didn't have long to wait; Millington Smythe came out into the street and set off at a brisk pace, Ben Doud followed at a safe distance; the infidel didn't bother to look round to see if he was being followed, he had become careless of late it seemed. They came to a small bus station on the Rua Lopes Quintas and Millington Smythe climbed aboard a number 23 bus. Ben Doud stopped at a newspaper stand at the entrance to the bus station and bought a paper; as he did so he heard the bus starting up and had to dash to get on. As he passed Millington Smythe he averted his face and continued to the back of the bus; sitting down he opened the paper pretending to read while he kept an eye on his victim. The bus wound it's way up the incline towards the Corcovado mountain, the road becoming steeper as they climbed and the elderly bus wheezed and groaned as the driver changed gears,

Millington Smythe was looking forward to viewing Rio from the top and also getting a close look at O Cristo Redenter, the huge 95 meter statue of Christ with its arms outstretched over the city. As the bus neared the top of the mountain they began to encounter low cloud, damn; thought Millington Smythe this cloud will spoil the view. He was right, as they pulled into the large car park there was a mist swirling around the top of the mountain. Everyone disembarked and began to follow the trail to the viewing point; it was hard to see more than a few yards in front of him and he stuck close to the rest of the passengers. An American tourist struck up a conversation with him as they arrived at the statue.

'Pity about this goldarned mist, I was hopin' to get some great shots of the statue and Rio to take home to the States.'

'Whereabouts are you from?' asked Millington Smythe politely.

'Why from God's own country; Dallas in the State of Texas, you're a Limey aint yer?'

171

'I'm English if that's what you mean,' he replied.

'I'm Hiram C. Goldfarb pleased to meet you,' he extended a ham like hand and Millington Smythe winced as his hand was grasped in a vice like grip, 'you here on holiday or business?'

Millington Smythe found the man's directness irritating, 'You will have to excuse me I am meeting someone and am overdue already.'

He turned on his heel and walked quickly away along the mountain path away from the Tourist site. The mist closed in like a cloak and he found it difficult to see ahead more than a few meters. Bin Doud had been hovering in the background whilst he had been talking with the American, now he saw his chance to catch Millington Smythe on his own. His hand slipped inside his coat and grasped the handle of the dagger, it felt comforting somehow.

172

CHAPTER FIFTY TWO

They walked hand in hand along the banks of Derwent Water, this was the second day of their honeymoon and it had been raining since they had arrived. However they were so absorbed with each other that it could have been snowing and they would not have cared. Cooper looked at Sheila as they walked, rain drops on her hair looked like small diamonds and seemed to enhance her complexion; he held her close as they strolled along the path..

'Do you fancy walking to the pub and having some lunch?'

She turned and looked up at him; 'Sounds like a good idea darling, I could eat a horse; there must be something in the air here I'm always hungry.'

'I doubt they will have horse on the menu Sheila, but we could probably share a small sheep or something.'

She pushed him playfully, 'are you ever serious Dan; you always turn everything in to a joke.'

A couple of grebe began to dance on the water carrying out their mating ritual; they stopped and watched the birds spellbound.

'I'm glad you didn't insist on us doing that before we got married, I can't swim that well,' said Cooper ducking as she swung her arm.

He ran off and she pursued him shouting, 'you wait Daniel Cooper till I catch up with you.'

He stopped and folded her in his arms, 'now what are you going to do to me Mrs. Cooper?'

She tilted her head and he kissed her tenderly, 'there that will have to do till we get back to the hotel.'

'Meany,' she said, 'I shall sue for divorce on grounds of mental cruelty.'

They linked arms and made their way towards the village drinking in the beauty of the Lakeland scenery.

He had not been so happy since his first marriage, in some ways this relationship seemed deeper than he had felt before. It wasn't that he had not had happy times with Angela; but this girl seemed to reach parts of his being that no one else had. They reached the old stone faced pub and entered the bar, it was full of tourists and locals alike and the sound of animated conversation.

'What would you like to drink,' he asked?

'I think I'll have a gin and tonic with a slice,' she answered, indicating a vacant table she made her way over and sat down.

He brought the drinks over and set them down, 'I'll get a menu and we'll see if they have a pony on there I don't think I could manage even half a horse.'

CHAPTER FIFTY THREE

The further Millington Smythe ventured along the stony path the rougher it got; the mist was getting thicker and he had no idea how near to the edge of the mountain he was. He decided to retrace his steps and return to the viewing area, at least there would be other people there and he didn't want to stay too long in these conditions. This venture had perhaps been a risk too far and he was now becoming very nervous realizing how vulnerable he had become. As he stumbled along the path a figure loomed out of the mist coming the other way, the man had his head down concentrating on the pathway until perhaps sensing someone else he looked up. On perceiving Millington Smythe the man stopped and stared at him; a look of recognition illuminated his face, then it changed to malevolence. Reaching inside his coat he removed a long curved knife and started towards him raising the knife as he came.

Millington Smythe stood transfixed in terror for a moment; then turning he began to run desperately back the way he had just come from. As he ran he was frantically trying to work out who had sent this man to kill him, perhaps he had been hired by the company in revenge for the scandal he had created. His breathing came in sobbing gasps as he began to slow down; he began to realize just how unfit he had become. He looked back, the man was slowly gaining on him; he redoubled his efforts and managed to draw away. In front of him loomed a rocky outcrop; fear lent him wings and he scrambled to the top dislodging loose scree as he climbed.

Standing there he looked down and beheld his adversary climbing after him; he picked up a large stone and hurled it, narrowly missing the man.

'What do you want of me,' he called out between gasps; 'who sent you?'

The man stopped and looking up said; 'Allah sent me to avenge my family and my tribe; you were responsible for their deaths.'

'I don't know what you are talking about.'

'In 1956 in Yemen you led a group of soldiers into the desert and attacked them leaving not one person alive, not even the children.'

'That was not me, I didn't lead them it was another soldier,' gasped Millington Smythe.

'You gave the orders for the attack so you have their blood on your hands and I am God's instrument of justice.'

As he spoke he was slowly moving forward towards his victim, suddenly he stood up and made a dash towards the cowering figure of Millington Smythe. Raising the knife he struck several times, as he did so his opponent grabbed him and held on; by this time they had reached the edge of the knoll and the loose rocks slid away. Loosing their footing they both plunged into the abyss; still locked together they hurtled down towards the Tijuca forest seven hundred meters below.

CHAPTER FIFTY FOUR

During the honeymoon they had discussed where they would live on returning to Norwich.

Cooper was eager to open the house up and rent out the flat.

Sheila was not so sure, 'don't you think there may be too many memories there for you darling?'

'No, because I'm putting you in charge of decorating the place, you can choose whatever wallpaper and paint you want.'

'I'm not too good with a paint brush and as for wall papering I get more paste on me than on the walls,' she said.

He drew her to him, 'I'm not suggesting that you should do it, get a tradesman in to do the heavy stuff, but you choose what you want; I'm renowned for having no design sense and I know you would hate whatever I chose.'

So it was agreed that the house was where they would finally move to; living temporarily in the flat until the house was ready.

On his return to work Foley updated him on the latest news regarding the death of Millington Smythe.

177

Cooper was silent for a moment, then he said; 'I think he was the victim of a Higher Justice than ours Foley, when you consider the number of lives he has affected by his actions.'

The Crown Oil Company had been rocked by the scandal; the papers had a great time digging out the whole story and the entire board had resigned. After the dust had settled there was much speculation in the Stock Market regarding a takeover and eventually it went to an American consortium of Gas and Petroleum companies. Life got back to what Cooper considered normal after the roller coaster of the Broadland killings; he became involved in the more mundane day to day criminal activities of the populace of Norfolk. Burglaries, domestic disputes and stolen tractors became the norm, he had time to share a domestic life with Sheila and their relationship blossomed into a deeper involvement. They moved into the now refurbished house where they became at ease with each other and happiness reigned supreme.

A year later their cup of contentment was filled to overflowing when Sheila produced their first child, a boy.

They argued over a name for him and finally settled on Lawrence, Daniel Cooper, the bearer of this impressive title made no comment other than to continue to suck his big toe.

'It's rather sad to think that he hasn't got any grandparents,' said Sheila wistfully, 'at least none that we know the whereabouts of.'

'You mean your mother,' remarked Cooper whose parents had both died some years ago, 'we could ask the Salvation Army to trace her, they are very good at finding people.'

'No, I think it would be a waste of time; she hasn't bothered to contact me in all these years so even if we managed to find her she probably wouldn't want to know.'

Many of his colleagues turned up for the Christening at the small local church, even the 'Super' put in an appearance.
Lawrence was a contented baby and only looked mildly surprised when the vicar anointed him. At the party afterwards everyone crowded round the star of the ceremony, Molly asked to hold him and was reluctant to return him to his mother'
'He's so good,' she cried, 'he didn't make a murmur during the service.'
'You should hear him when he wants his feed at two in the morning,' laughed Sheila, "he certainly has a sturdy pair of lungs.'

A week later Chief Superintendent Trafford sent for Cooper; 'I wonder what he wants to see me about;' he remarked to Foley.
'Haven't a clue,' the Cadet replied, 'you haven't left your car in his space or something equally sacrilegious have you?'
Cooper thumbed his nose at him and went up to the 'Super's' office, he knocked and went in.
'Ah, come in Cooper good to see you, take a seat,' he seemed in a particularly affable mood this morning.
He picked up a file and looked benevolently at Cooper; 'you may be aware that Inspector Grant is retiring this year Cooper and I shall be looking for a suitable replacement.' Cooper's heart sank, he could guess what was coming and he had been dreading it.
'After careful consideration and discussion with the Chief Constable and with particular reference to your excellent

detective work during the Broadland case we felt that you would be our first choice to fill the vacancy.'

He looked expectantly at Cooper, who was studying the floor, a frown crossed the 'Super's' face, 'well man; what have you got to say?'
'I am well aware of the honour of the promotion and your faith in me sir, but I must be honest and decline the promotion.'
'For God's sake why Cooper?' exclaimed Trafford.
'I love the job I do sir; field work is where I feel comfortable, sitting at a desk all day dealing with masses of paperwork would be anathema to me.' 'People and what makes them tick is meat and drink to me sir and I thrive on it; detection of crime gives me all the job satisfaction I need.'
The Superintendent sat back in his chair and looked at him in disbelief; 'you mean you don't want to progress in the Service; this is a once in a lifetime opportunity which will mean a large increase in your salary and status.'
'Surely as a newly married man these benefits would make life easier for you and your wife and family?'

Cooper leaned forward and looked him in the eye.
'With all due respect sir I have found my niche in the Police Force; I'm happy with the work I do and have no wish to change.'
The 'Super' frowned; 'well I must say that I find your attitude disappointing Cooper, I had you down as a suitable candidate for advancement, however if that is your answer I must respect it, but you must realize that the offer will not be made again.'

'I do sir and I thank you for considering me,' Cooper smiled as he stood up to leave; he looked and felt as if a great weight had been lifted from him.

He arrived home that evening in a reflective mood wondering how Sheila would react when she learned that he had turned down the promotion.

He needn't have worried, when he told her his reasons she said, 'I'm glad you stuck to your guns Dan, a lesser man would have accepted just to please his superior and then been unhappy.' 'You have found a job that makes you feel fulfilled; there are a lot of people in this world that never do.' Putting her arm through his and laying her head on his shoulder she said, 'besides I prefer you as you are.'

He kissed her and said, 'good! Now what's my son and heir been up to today?'

Printed in Great Britain
by Amazon